Claudia's Book

Other books by
Ann M. Martin

Rachel Parker, Kindergarten Show-off
Eleven Kids, One Summer
Ma and Pa Dracula
Yours Turly, Shirley
Ten Kids, No Pets
Slam Book
Just a Summer Romance
Missing Since Monday
With You and Without You
Me and Katie (the Pest)
Stage Fright
Inside Out
Bummer Summer

BABY-SITTERS LITTLE SISTER series
THE BABY-SITTERS CLUB mysteries
THE BABY-SITTERS CLUB series

Claudia's Book

Ann M. Martin

SCHOLASTIC INC.
New York Toronto London Auckland Sydney

Interior art and cover drawing by Angelo Tillery

Cover painting by Hodges Soileau

ISBN 0-590-48400-1

12 11 10 9 8 7 6 5 4 3 2 1 5 6 7 8 9/9 0/0

Printed in the U.S.A. 40

First Scholastic printing, March 1995

The author gratefully acknowledges
Nola Thacker
for her help in
preparing this manuscript.

I looked down at the blank sheet of paper on my desk. I leaned back and looked up at the ceiling. I turned and looked out the window.

Mistake. Through my windows I could see trees and clouds and the roofs of houses. In the distance, a v-shaped flock of geese flew by. Even further above that I caught the glint of light off a plane.

All of which reminded me that I'd rather be anywhere than right there at my desk getting ready to do my math homework. And then there was more homework after that, including a BIG writing project. . . .

But as usual, I'm jumping into the middle of things. I guess that's because I see things not as having a beginning and an end, but as a big picture spreading out all around me with me (of course) at the center.

Me? I'm Claudia. Claudia Kishi. I'm thirteen years old. I live in Stoneybrook with my parents and my older sister Janine. Janine is a genius. A real genius. I'm not kidding. Even though she's only in high school, she's already taking college courses because the high school stuff is too easy for her. Janine's idea of an exciting afternoon is probably doing advanced college calculus.

Not me. I'm in eighth grade at Stoneybrook Middle School and I'm not a great student, like Janine. It's not simply that I don't like doing homework (who does—except Janine?), it's that I'm not very good at spelling and writing and math. I'm smart, but, well, school and I (except for art and maybe phys ed) just don't agree.

My poor parents don't get it. My father is a lawyer and my mother is a librarian and they love books and writing and words, and they don't always understand the way I see the world. But they're getting used to the idea of having an artist for a daughter.

Because that's what I am good at: art. Maybe that explains why I see things as a whole picture all at once, an image. Sometimes, when you're an artist, you see just a fuzzy, vague sort of image at first and it becomes more clear as you work. Other times, you know exactly what you want to create and then the hard part is making your art match what you see in your head.

Math and English and spelling don't exactly work that way.

I looked back down at my desk. What I saw was a piece of notebook paper with a stack of parallel blue lines. I could imagine all kinds of possibilities for that piece of paper, possibilities involving color and shape and angles and shadows.

What I couldn't imagine was my math homework.

That's when I decided to call Stacey McGill. Who is Stacey? She's my best friend, fellow officer in the Baby-sitters Club (more about that a little later), and resident SMS math whiz.

Her line was busy. I sighed and hung up the phone. I stared longingly at my art supplies, but gave myself a good mental shake. If I started an art project, I might not even remember to call Stacey back and then I'd never start my homework.

I also said no to the Nancy Drew books hidden around my room (behind the "recommended" books my mother and father approve of). But I said yes to a snack.

Because I also have, well, an appreciation for what some people call junk food. But then, some people call wonderful works of art junk, too, right? Even Nancy Drew books! It's all in how you look at it.

I got up and fished around in the pocket of

my good winter coat (I only wear it on special occasions, so the pockets are a great place in which to "store" things). Sure enough, I'd stored a Fruit Roll-Up in one pocket and a tiny packet of Hershey's Hugs in the other.

I returned to my desk, sat down, and opened the Fruit Roll-Up. Of course, that wasn't the only junk food hidden around my room. I keep a large supply handy because I am the vice-president of the BSC and the meetings are held in my room. I'm the only member with my own phone line, so we can use the phone without having to worry about tying up the line so other people can't use it. So I furnish the room, the phone, and the junk food.

Besides Stacey, five fellow officers and good friends of mine are in the BSC.

Kristy Thomas is the president of the club, because she's the one who started it (one of her many great ideas). If there were an Olympic event in organization, Kristy would be winner and world champion. She's also very responsible and has no problem making herself heard, which is a good thing since she lives in a very large family with two older brothers, one younger brother, one adopted sister, one stepsister, one stepbrother, a mother, a stepfather, a grandmother, a dog, a cranky cat, two goldfish, *and* (some of the younger kids in the family believe) a resident ghost. In addition to all that, Kristy is the captain of a kids' softball team called Kristy's Krushers.

The secretary of the BSC (and Kristy's best friend) is Mary Anne Spier. Like Kristy, Mary Anne is short (although Kristy is the shortest kid in our class) and lives in an extended family. (Her mother died when Mary Anne was just a baby, and she and her father were a two-person family for a long time.) Mary Anne is also very organized. One of her jobs as the BSC secretary is to keep up to date the club record book with all our appointments in it, and she's never, ever made a mistake. But while Kristy is outspoken, Mary Anne is shy and very sensitive. Don't make the mistake of thinking that Mary Anne is a pushover because she is shy, though. Mary Anne can be just as stubborn as Kristy — maybe even more so.

Mary Anne's extended family includes another member of the BSC: Dawn Schafer. Dawn moved to Stoneybrook, where her mother had grown up, with her mom and brother after her parents were divorced. After Mary Anne and Dawn became friends and discovered the fascinating parental fact that their parents had dated in high school, they naturally decided that Mr. Spier and Mrs. Schafer had to get together again. The result: a wedding. And now Mary Anne and her father live in this cool old farmhouse (that might be haunted) with Dawn and her mother, making Dawn Mary Anne's best friend (along with Kristy) *and* her sister. Dawn is the alternate officer of the BSC. That means she takes over the duties of any BSC officer who can't make a meeting. I think of Dawn whenever I eat junk food, because Dawn never lets the stuff touch her lips. She thinks sugar is disgusting. I still haven't made up my mind about the tofu she eats. I actually like Tofutti, which is a sort of ice cream made of tofu. And Dawn, who is tall and has long, pale blonde hair and piercing blue eyes, *is* a good argument for healthy food — if being smart and laid-back and looking totally together is the result of all those sprouts and tofu!

Jessi Ramsey is one of our two junior officers. (The junior officers are in sixth grade, and can't baby-sit at night yet, except for their own families.) Like Dawn, Jessi is tall and slender. She has black hair and warm brown eyes. But if you look at Jessi carefully, you can tell by the way she stands (and by the way she often wears her hair pulled back in a bun) that she is studying to be a ballet dancer. She gets up every morning at five-thirty to practice, and she takes lessons several times a week. Pretty awesome.

Mallory Pike, the other junior officer, couldn't be more different in some ways than her best friend Jessi. Mal has red hair and freckles and wears glasses and braces. And it's not that she is uncoordinated, but she's not particularly athletic either. Being the oldest of eight kids (three of her brothers are *triplets*) makes her an excellent baby-sitter. It's also given her a headstart on what she wants to do someday: write and illustrate children's books. Meanwhile, she enjoys the relative calm of Jessi's family (which is made up of two parents, one aunt, and Jessi's younger sister and brother) and Jessi enjoys the high energy of the Pikes. Differences aside, Jessi and Mal have a lot in common. They share a love of mysteries, for example. And they both love horses.

Of course, I saved the best for last — my best friend and the BSC treasurer, Stacey.

I had never had a best friend before Stacey moved to Stoneybrook from New York. And when Stacey's parents moved back to New York after Stacey and I had become best friends, it was awful. So while I wasn't glad when Stacey's parents later got divorced, I was totally pleased when Stacey and her mom returned to Stoneybrook.

Stacey is a math whiz and, like Dawn (but not me), she watches what she eats. Stacey has to. She has diabetes, a disease that makes it hard for her body to handle sugar. She has to be very careful about what she eats (she can't have sugar) and even has to give herself insulin injections every day. If she isn't careful, she could get very sick. Stacey takes it all in stride. When we hang out together, she munches on apples and pretzels while I go on Mallomar binges.

Stacey and I are about the same height and we have long hair, but hers is blonde. She is also a super cool, New York-style dresser, and probably the most sophisticated girl in SMS. She sometimes wears a lot of black (it's a New York City thing) and always looks as if she knows exactly where she's going and how to get there.

And besides being smart and elegant and a true blue loyal best friend, she's excellent at explaining math things.

Math . . . sigh.

I reached for the phone again. This time Stacey answered.

"Hi," I said. "Math." (I didn't have to tell her who it was.)

"Hold on," she replied. A moment later, she was going over the questions with me. By the time we were through, she'd helped me figure out how to solve the problems. But we didn't hang up immediately. Instead, even though we'd seen each other at school that day, we planned a shopping trip to the mall over the weekend.

And we talked about our latest assignment for school: to write our autobiographies. Stacey was thrilled with the project. I wasn't — although I admitted to Stacey that I *had* been looking through my baby book and going through boxes of old stuff that my mom and dad had saved from when Janine and I were kids.

"I'm remembering the weirdest things," I said. "Like the time I drew all over the bathroom walls and then tried to convince my mom it was an art show."

Stacey cracked up. "Hey, you were doing something that was very in. Remember that art gallery owner in New York who had one of her first shows in *her* bathroom?"

I'd forgotten about that. I grinned. "Yeah . . . anyway, my parents and my sister are remembering these little-kid embarrassing things which I am *not* going to put in writing anywhere."

"Tell me about it," said Stacey. "But wait till you start writing, Claud. You're going to get into it."

"Maybe," I said.

"It's a self-portrait with words," Stacey pointed out.

I thought about that for a moment. I liked the idea. I told Stacey so. Then we talked a little while longer about important things, such as what we were going to wear the next day.

I hung up and finished my homework (including my math).

Then I looked at myself in the mirror. A self-portrait with words. When I was in kindergarten and the teacher told us to draw a self-portrait, I'd drawn a butterfly. I was the only kid who had not drawn a literal portrait of herself: two eyes, a nose, a mouth.

My self-portrait had been different then (I still have it, and I still like it). Looking back at me from the mirror wasn't a butterfly: just Claudia Kishi, with long black hair and brown eyes and an enormous shirt and patchwork vest over striped leggings. I looked down at my high-tops and back at the earrings I was wearing. I'd made them myself out of leftover bits of broken jewelry that my friends and family had given me: patchwork earrings.

I was still wearing butterfly colors. Maybe the kindergarten Claud was even smarter than she'd realized.

I went back to my desk, sat down, and pulled my notebook toward me.

An Artists Life
by Claudia Kishi

Baby days

I was born on July 11th in Stoneybrook Connectticut. The anouncement of my birth was in the stoneybrook Gazett a newspaper that is not in bussiness any more. I have lived in a house on Bradford Court all my life . . .

Baby days

BIRTH ANNOUNCEMENTS

Mr. John and Mrs. Rioko Kishi are proud to announce the arrival of their daughter, Claudia Lynn Kishi, 7 lbs., 7 oz., on July 11th at Stoneybrook General Hospital in Stoneybrook, Conn. Claudia is the sister of Janine Kishi and the granddaughter of Mrs. Mimi Yamamoto also of Stoneybrook, Conn.

It's a gril!

I don't remember being born, of course, but my mother and father do because they were *both* there (of course, my mother had to be there). My father said I started "expressing myself creatively the moment I was born." My mother says it's true: I started yelling when the doctor held me up and told my parents, "You have a beautiful baby girl."

I don't remember coming home from the hospital and I don't remember my first meeting with the person in our family I looked most like when I was born (and look most like now), my grandmother, Mimi. Mimi had stayed home to take care of my older sister Janine, who was three and a half at the time.

I wish Mimi were still alive, so I could ask her about that meeting. There are a million things I wish I could ask her. I miss her every day. She always understood me and she was the person I was closest to in our family. She called me "my Claudia." I have a picture of Mimi when she was twelve and a picture of me when I was twelve. I matted them and framed them together and they are hanging over my desk while I am writing this. I miss her, my Mimi.

I asked my sister if she remembered the first time she met me. And although my sister was only three and a half, she remembered.

I knocked on the door of Janine's room. I knew she was inside, probably corresponding with Mars on her computer. I could hear her tapping away. It took her a long time to stop tapping and say, "Come in." I guess she was pretty focused on what she was doing.

I went in. "May I sit down?" I asked.

Janine looked a little surprised to see me, but she nodded and I plopped down in her chair. I'd brought my notebook with me and I flipped it open. "I'd like to ask you a few questions," I said.

Janine looked even more surprised. She took her hands off the keyboard and folded them in her lap. She straightened her shoulders and stared at me seriously. I wondered if this was

Baby days

how she takes tests or sits in interviews. (My sister has won a million awards for being a genius and has been written up in the newspaper a gazillion times since her own birth announcement.)

"To what do these questions pertain?" she asked.

She talks like that, too. But I'm used to it. I knew she meant: what was I going to ask her about?

"No sweat," I assured her. "We have to write our autobiographies for school and I wondered if you remembered when I came home from the hospital."

Janine relaxed — a little. And she smiled — sort of. She tilted her head and thought for a long moment. Then she said, "Yes."

"Could you tell me what you remember?"

"Yes," said Janine again. "It was in the early afternoon. Mimi and I had just finished lunch. We were having my favorite lunch at the time: alphabet soup and I had found all of the alphabet except y and z."

Good grief, I thought.

"Mimi was trying to teach me how to spell 'Claudia' with the alphabet letters when we heard mom and dad pull into the driveway. A minute later, they came in through the side door, holding you."

Me and mom just got home from the hospitel.
My first meeting with Mimi.
And Janine, too, of course.

"You remember all that?" I exclaimed, taking notes as fast as I could.

Janine nodded. "Of course. You were in a green blanket. Mom handed you to Mimi and Mimi looked at you and said, 'My Claudia.' "

I felt sudden tears sting my eyes. I bent over and pretended to erase something in my notebook. Janine paused for a moment, too, and cleared her throat.

Then she went on. "It was a sunny day. I remember that because we went outside and Dad took a picture of Mom, Mimi, me, and you together. Then I went back inside with Mimi and she told me I would have to be a good example for my new sister. So I ate all the letters in the alphabet letters and then I finished my soup."

Janine unfolded her hands and turned back to her computer.

"That's it?" I asked.

"Yes," said Janine, her fingers poised above her keyboard. "To the best of my recollection."

"Thanks," I said.

Mimi was my first best friend, really, before Stacey. But my first two friends were Kristy and Mary Anne, who lived next door to each other across the street from me. I don't remember the first time we all met. I know our parents used to take turns taking care of the three of us even when we were pretty little.

But one of my earliest memories involves Kristy and Mary Anne. We were about four and a half or five and my folks had just had our driveway changed from gravel to cement. And they were having a little cement walkway made in the backyard.

We were fascinated by everything: the cement trucks, the tools, the way the guys putting the cement down kept smoothing it back and forth. We'd been playing with trucks and making cement mixer sounds in the sandbox in a corner of the yard.

Anyway, that day, they'd finished the walkway and had put up strings with strips of white cloth tied to them so nobody would walk on the wet walk by accident.

And of course, the moment we heard that you could leave permanent footprints in the cement, we were even more fascinated. We knew we wouldn't be allowed to do this, so we didn't ask about it.

Instead, we sat under a tree in the backyard, playing in the sandbox (Kristy had a toy dump truck that actually made beep, beep, beep sounds when it was dumping its cargo, of which I was deeply envious), while Mimi worked in the garden nearby. After awhile, Mimi pushed her straw hat back, wiped her-forehead, and asked us if we wanted something to drink.

We said no. We nodded when Mimi said she would be right back and agreed that we would stay where we were. Then we kept playing while Mimi checked the back gate to make sure it was locked so we couldn't get out.

And the moment the back door closed we practically flew across the yard to the wet cement.

"Look!" I said, leaning over. I drew my fingers through the cement. I still remember how it felt: wet and gritty. I wondered if it would taste sandy and crunchy (maybe I liked junk food even then!). I wiggled my fingers and made four wavy lines in the cement.

Kristy knelt down and drew the fingers of *both* her hands through the cement.

Mary Anne stood there for a moment, looking worried. But she could not resist it. She leaned over and stuck her fingers into the cement and made four deep holes. "Euuuuw," she said, giggling and pulling her fingers out.

In no time at all we'd decorated a huge section of sidewalk with our "art." About the only thing we didn't do was walk in the wet cement. We were afraid our shoes would stick in it, and we didn't think to take them off.

We'd completely forgotten about our sandbox and about Mimi when a soft voice said, "Claudia! What are you doing?"

We all jumped about a mile.

I turned to face Mimi. It was hard to tell what she was thinking. I stared down at the sidewalk. There was barely a smooth square inch on it. Uh-oh.

"We're making pictures," I said at last.

"I wrote my name," said Kristy, pointing at the giant letters at the end of the sidewalk.

Mary Anne's face got very red. She said, "I drew on the sidewalk, too."

Mimi looked at us. She looked at the side-walk. We knew we were in trouble.

"Did you really think this was the place to draw pictures?" Mimi asked me.

I hung my head. "No," I confessed. "I'm sorry."

"Me too," said Kristy.

"Me too," said Mary Anne.

Mimi thought for a moment. Then she nodded. She took us in the house and washed our hands. Then she made a phone call.

A little while later (when we were in the backyard again, in the sandbox, at a safe distance from our "art") one of the workmen returned and smoothed over the sidewalk. When he finished, he called, "All done." He looked at us and grinned.

"I thank you," said Mimi in her soft, polite voice. She led us to the end of the walkway by the back door steps. "Now," she said, "you may each lean over and put your hands in the cement, here."

We stood there for a moment in shock. We couldn't believe we were going to be allowed to play in the cement again.

Mimi smiled and nodded. She leaned over and spread her hands out and held them just above the surface of the wet cement. "Like this," she said. "And press down carefully."

"Wow," said Kristy. She leaned over and pressed her hands into the wet cement. Giggling, Mary Anne and I followed suit.

"Now lift your hands straight up," said Mimi.

We lifted our hands up. When we did, we left a neat row of hand prints, six in all, along one side of the walk.

"Now you can see how you grow," said Mimi, smiling.

And we did. For a long time after the walkway dried, we put our hands in the prints almost every day to see if we were growing. When Kristy's little brother David Michael turned four, she brought him over and let him fit his hands into the prints.

Mary Anne and Kristy have both moved to

new neighborhoods. We've all grown up. But I still stop when I go down the back walk and check the prints. I can't believe I was ever that little.

It was a pretty cool day.

Happy Birthday To Me

What if you had a birthday party and no body came? It would be pretty majorly tramatic, huh? It was for me. It hapened when I was turning six years old. I'd made these beatiful invitations to give to every body in my kindergarden class at Stoneybrook Ellementery school....

I liked kindergarten. I liked it the first day I saw it. I wasn't scared the way some kids were. (Cokie Mason put her hands on her hips and stomped her foot and told her father to "Stay right where you are!" when he started to leave her. I remember I was completely shocked that a little kid could talk to a grown-up like that.)

But Mimi had brought me to school the first day (Mr. Spier had given us a ride), and Kristy and her mom were there when we arrived, so it wasn't any big deal. Kristy, I remember, looked around the room, folded her arms, and said, "Not bad." Mary Anne looked a little teary-eyed when her father started to leave, but before she could work up a cry, Kristy was saying, "The teacher said we get our own cubbies. We better go pick out the good ones." Kristy had already scoped out the cubby situation (her older brothers had explained about them to her) and she took us straight to the cubbies near the windows and told us they were the best. By the time she'd showed us how to put our coats and lunches and stuff in our cubbies, our parents had left and Mrs. Kushel was calling us to the middle of the room for a hello song.

We had a big open classroom that was lined

with windows on one side, the wall of cubbies across the back of the room. We had a bulletin board above the cubbies and on the other side of the room across from the cubbies were low bookshelves and cabinets with more bulletin boards above that. At the front of the room was a big blackboard and the teacher's desk.

My cubby was next to Kristy's, and Mary Anne's was on the other side. We'd been the first to choose our cubbies, and all the girls had picked out cubbies on one side, while the boys had taken the cubbies on the other side. We had an aquarium and a terrarium and a giant jigsaw puzzle on a low table in one corner of the room that we could work on in free time. (I was very good at the jigsaw puzzle. I like to match the colors and make the pictures.)

So I was pretty cool about my first day of school, thanks to Kristy and Mary Anne. And I liked the other kids, or most of them anyway. Alan Gray and Pete Black were in my class, too, along with Cokie Mason, and we're still together in eighth grade at SMS.

You know, it's funny, but I don't remember how any of us looked. I mean, in my mind, we all looked just the same then as we do now. And some of us *are* pretty much the same, come to think of it. Alan learned that trick of rolling his eyes all the way back in his head so just the whites showed, back when we were in kindergarten. He still does it now and it still grosses me out.

But the class picture of my kindergarten shows something very, very different! We were all either cute or goofy-looking. (In that picture, my hair was in pigtails and I was wearing double ribbons on each pigtail — four colors in all — to match the flowered blouse I was wearing with my purple Oshkosh overalls. I think I had purple sneakers, too.)

Kindergarten was cool, though. Mrs. Kushel, our teacher, seemed really old to me. She had blonde hair, dangling down in tight ringlets and tended to shout at our class. I didn't like that, but since I didn't usually get into trouble the way Alan or Kristy did (except that I had a hard time keeping still and paying attention to anything for very long), it wasn't too bad. And we had art class. The art teacher, Miss Packett, wasn't very good (I know now) not only because she played favorites, but because her favorite art projects were dull: coloring in the lines, making sure the colors matched. She lined up a row of apples once — including a green apple — and we were supposed to color them as close to the colors we saw as possible. But I got carried away and made a row of apples in all the primary colors. Miss Packett didn't like *that* one bit. But all

Me, Kristy, and Mary Ann in kindergardin.
Prakticaly grown up!

she said was, "Very interesting, Claudia."

Janine, of course, had aced kindergarten and was even doing some fourth-grade stuff although she was only in third grade. I walked to school every morning with Kristy and Mary Anne. (My job was to go get them first). We would return to my house where Janine would be waiting to walk us to school. If it was a nice day, she'd wait outside on the front steps, reading. If it was a rainy or cold or snowy day, she'd wait just inside the door — reading. Then she'd walk behind us all the way to school. Guess what she was doing while she was walking? Reading.

That was okay with us. We had plenty to talk about: whether trading lunches (Mary Anne's father always called after her as she was leaving not to trade her lunch at school) meant the whole lunch or if Mary Anne could swap an apple for a banana with me or for an orange with Kristy; whether Alan Gray really had seen a giant boa constrictor in the bushes at the edge of the playground . . . you get the idea.

And that June, during the very last week of kindergarten, I had something really, really important to talk about: my sixth birthday party. It was less than a month away and my parents had told me I could have a big party and invite the *whole* kindergarten class. I was very excited. Plus, I had talked them into letting me help plan it, and they had agreed and had let me choose the theme for it.

I had chosen the circus. I adored circuses back then. I wanted to be a lion tamer. I loved how brave they looked and I loved the cool clothes they wore.

So we were going to serve hot dogs and popcorn and peanuts and ice cream just like at the circus, and Mimi had helped me make these neat invitations that looked like tickets to the circus and said, "Admit One Guest to Claudia's Birthday Circus Celebration." Underneath it explained that I was having a circus-themed birthday party and when and where and my phone number to RSVP, which I thought was really grown-up when I found out the letters stood for French words that meant to please call and say whether you were coming or not.

"And guess what," I said dramatically, as we were walking to kindergarten on the very last day of school. I'd been saying that about a million times a day for the past few days, but my friends didn't let me down.

"What?" asked Kristy and Mary Anne together.

"My father's going to get real clown face paint and paint our faces like clowns!"

"Ooooh," said Mary Anne. Then she

frowned worriedly. "What if my father won't let me because it's messy?"

That stopped me for a moment. Then I said, "Tell him you need to wear old clothes so that if you do get clown makeup on them, it'll be okay."

"Also, you can put aprons over everybody before they get their faces painted, Claudia," said Kristy (a world-class organizer even then). "Ask your mom or dad for one of their old kitchen aprons."

"That's a great idea," I said admiringly. I reached inside my bookbag and patted the stack of invitations lovingly. I could hardly wait to give them out. My parents had been planning to mail them, but I'd talked them into letting me hand them out at school, so I'd be *sure* everyone got one.

But it was hard to find just the right time to do it on the last day of school. Mrs. Kushel started the class by letting people talk about what they were going to do over summer vacation. Then our class gave Mrs. Kushel a big thank-you card that we'd made in art class with Miss Packett's help. (She'd drawn a picture of the school with the words "SES Kindergarten Class" and the date on the outside.) We all got to color a little of it — in the lines and in the right colors, of course. Inside we'd printed our names.

Mrs. Kushel thanked us calmly, which was pretty amazing because everyone was mega-excited and racing around. Kristy and Cokie Mason had a fight on the playground, I remember, because Cokie thought Kristy had deliberately tripped her while they were jumping rope and Kristy said Cokie was just clumsy. And Alan had put Vaseline on his hand and kept shaking hands with everybody and making them shriek until Mrs. Kushel caught him (actually, Alan asked her to shake hands and she did). It was pretty wild.

Then after lunch (when Mrs. Kushel handed out cupcakes to each of us for dessert) we held an awards ceremony. Kids got awards for all kinds of things: neatest cubby and best attendance and never being late, and the kids who didn't get those kinds of awards got good citizenship awards (I got one of those). Finally, at the very end of the day we had to clean out our cubbies.

And then suddenly the last bell rang. I was crouched in front of my cubby, holding my invitations, and I jumped straight up in the air.

"Wait a minute!" I shouted. I gave a handful of invitations to Kristy and a handful of them to Mary Anne. "Quick," I told them. "Give everyone an invitation."

Kristy raced to the door of the classroom with hers and started giving them to the kids who were already headed for the door. I ran around the room, handing mine out.

Alan took his and said, "What's this, a report card?"

"No, silly," I told him. "It's an invitation to my birthday party in July. It's a circus party."

"Neat," said Alan, cramming the card into his backpack without even opening it.

Cokie looked at hers and said, "We're going to the beach. All summer. Do you want your invitation back?"

"You can keep it." I wasn't too disappointed that Cokie couldn't come.

I ended up with two invitations left over, but then I remembered that we'd made extra ones and that I was going to give one to my teacher, too.

I grabbed my bookbag out of my cubby and joined Mary Anne and Kristy by the door.

"Here," I said to Mrs. Kushel.

"Another card?" she said. "How nice, Claudia . . ."

At that moment, a chair crashed over and Mrs. Kushel had to stop Alan and Pete from playing tag.

"Are you coming or not?" said a bored voice, and I looked up to see Janine waiting for us in the hall.

"Did you guys hand out all your invitations?" I asked Mary Anne and Kristy worriedly. "Do you think Mrs. Kushel will read hers?"

"Of course she will," said Kristy. "I handed out all of mine."

"All but one," said Mary Anne. "And I *might* have given someone an invitation twice."

"That's okay," I said. "There were extras."

"Claudia!" said Janine.

"Okay, okay." We started walking down the hall. I leaned over to my friends and whispered, "My sister acts just like Mrs. Kushel."

We looked back at my sister. She'd stuck a pencil behind her ear and was twirling her hair into ringlets like Mrs. Kushel.

We burst out laughing. Kindergarten was over and we were practically grown-up first-graders and summer was going to be great — especially my birthday party.

My mom was worried, though. I realize that, now that I'm older. She asked me several times, as the day of my birthday party drew closer, if I was sure I had given out all the invitations.

"Of course I'm sure," I said. I didn't even think about it. The summer had been *endless* so far. Wasn't my birthday *ever* going to come?

"No one's called to say whether they're coming," Mom said.

"Kristy and Mary Anne have," I replied. "And I told you that Cokie can't come." I stopped and frowned, remembering what had happened when I'd given my invitation to my teacher. "And I don't think Mrs. Kushel is coming, either."

My mother looked thoughtful. "Well, it *is* summer," said my mother. "I know people have all kinds of plans. And Mimi could have forgotten to write RSVP on the invitations, or at least on some of them . . ."

I wasn't listening. If I had been, I might have told my mom that I clearly recalled that "RSVP" — looking very cool and sophisticated and grown-up — was written across the bottom of every invitation. But I had already spun away.

"You won't forget to order the cake?" I demanded breathlessly. It was a special ice-cream birthday cake from King Kone's, a store in Stoneybrook that specialized in ice-cream cakes made to order. Mine was going to be a circus cake, with circus decorations on top.

"I won't forget," my mother promised.

And she didn't. She let me go with her the morning of the party to pick up the cake. It was beautiful. Like the Calder circus mobile at the Whitney Museum in New York. And right in the middle of the cake was a lion tamer with long black hair — me!

I was so excited. My mother smiled, and the guy behind the counter said, "Happy birthday, circus girl — or do I mean happy circus, birthday girl?" Then he reminded my mom to let the cake thaw out in the refrigerator and not to wait too long to serve it or it would begin to melt.

When we got back home I raced upstairs to

change into my party outfit. Even though it was summer, I was wearing black tights and my tall black rainboots and my red jacket with the brass buttons. I had a T-shirt with a lion's head painted on the front and I wore that under the jacket. I thought it made me look like a lion tamer.

I was standing in front of the mirror admiring my outfit when Janine stopped in the doorway of my room. She was wearing a Laura Ashley flowered dress and white tights and flats. She frowned. "That's not a birthday outfit," she said.

"It is for *my* birthday," I replied firmly.

Janine looked as if she were about to say more, but then Mimi appeared behind her. "You look very nice, my granddaughters," she said. She smiled. "Now we must help your parents finish making the house ready for the party."

We went downstairs and I stopped in the door of the dining room. My mouth dropped open. It had been transformed.

Crepe paper streamers of every color had been tied to the hanging light above the dining room table, then stretched out to the corners of the room, turning it into a sort of tent. Circus paper plates were laid out on a circus paper tablecloth. My father was arranging forks and spoons and circus napkins on the table.

My mother bustled in carrying a rolled-up piece of paper and a shoebox. I recognized it immediately. We were going to play a circus version of pin the tail on the donkey called "pin the nose on the clown." I'd helped my mom cut out the round red clown noses to go on the picture of the laughing clown's face my mom had found in a poster shop.

"Good. There you are," she said. She looked at her watch. "The guests will be here any minute. Janine, why don't you put this poster up outside on the back wall of the garage."

"Claudia and I will get the cups for the punch," said Mimi.

"The *three-ring* punch," I said (Mom had cut rings of orange, lemon, and lime to float in the bright red punch).

"The first game I'm going to play is circus Simon says," I told Mimi excitedly as we set out the punch bowl and cups. "The things I will say will be circus things. You know, 'circus Simon says, roar like a lion.' "

Mimi nodded. The doorbell rang.

"I'll get it!" I shrieked and raced to the front door.

It was Kristy and Mary Anne. They were in their party clothes. That meant that Mary

Anne was wearing a pink flowered dress with pink tights and flat black patent leather shoes. Her hair was fixed in pigtails and tied with pink bows. She was holding a neatly wrapped package.

Kristy was wearing navy blue shorts with a matching camp shirt, white socks, and her best sneakers. Her package was also neatly wrapped and she thrust it into my hands before I could say anything.

"Happy birthday, Claudia," she cried, and charged in.

"Happy birthday," Mary Anne echoed, giving me my present and walking with me into the house.

Kristy stopped in her tracks at the sight of the dining room. "Wooow," she said. "Neat and *awesome*, Claudia."

"Would you like some refreshments?" asked Janine, who'd taken up a position by the punch bowl.

"Double yes," said Kristy.

"Yes, please," said Mary Anne.

Janine ladled out the punch. She even ladled me out some when I asked, I guess because it was my birthday. She gave punch to Mom, Dad, and Mimi and then poured a cup for herself.

My father cleared his throat. "Well, we'll be singing 'Happy Birthday' soon, but let me take this opportunity to say it." He raised his punch. "Happy birthday, Claudia."

"Thank you," I said. I had put the gifts on the side table in the dining room. I kept looking at them. What was inside? I could hardly wait to open them. Maybe we would play one — no, two — games and then I'd open the gifts. Or maybe it would be better to play all the games and open the gifts last, while we had punch and ice-cream cake.

We finished the punch. My mother looked at her watch. "It's almost twelve-thirty," she said. The invitation said the party started at twelve. "I'm surprised people are so late."

"Summertime is different from regular time," my father said. "People take things more slowly in the summer."

"True," said my mother. "Let me go check on the cake." She disappeared into the kitchen.

"Want to go see the pin the nose on the clown?" I asked Kristy and Mary Anne. Of course they did. So we went outside and admired that.

Then we ran back inside.

"More punch?" asked Janine.

"No, thank you," I said. "I want to save some for when the others get here."

We waited.

And waited.

My mother looked at her watch again. "It's one o'clock," she said finally. "I don't think anyone else is coming."

"But they *have* to!" I burst out. "It's my birthday!"

"Are you sure you gave out all the invitations?" asked my father.

"Yes! Kristy and Mary Anne helped me!" I could feel a lump in my throat. Why wasn't anyone at my birthday party?

"Maybe people forgot," said Kristy. "Like maybe because it was the last day of school and they forgot to show the invitations to their parents."

Mary Anne added, "We gave them out right at the end of the day."

She and Kristy and I all began to talk at once, telling how we'd given out the invitations and who we remembered giving them to and what people had said. At last my mother held up her hand. "Okay, okay. Hold on. You know what I think?" She checked her watch one more time and sighed. "I think half of those kids forgot to show their parents the invitations in all the excitement of the last day of school. The other half are probably on vacation and forgot. And maybe Mimi did forget to write RSVP on some invitations."

"You mean no one's coming to my party?"

I cried. Tears began to sting the backs of my eyelids.

"I'm afraid not," said my mother.

"We're here! Me and Mary Anne," Kristy said.

"And the three of you can have a party anyway," said Janine. She looked almost as upset as I felt. That just made it worse — that my older sister felt *sorry* for me. "You open the presents and I'll go get the cake."

"I'll help you light the candles," said my mom.

I didn't say anything. I was trying hard not to cry. I was being brave.

Janine and Mom were gone for what seemed a long time. When they came back, Janine was holding the cake. The candles — seven in all, six and one to grow on — were arranged around the lion tamer, burning brightly. Janine and my mom began to sing "Happy Birthday to You" as they came into the room and everyone quickly joined in.

But I didn't blow out the candles on the cake. I watched as they sagged lower and lower while everyone sang. I watched as they sank into the melting, soggy ice-cream cake. I watched as one drowned in the ice cream and went out with a nasty burnt milk smell. I watched as the little lion tamer figure on top fell over in the goo that was my melted birthday cake.

And then I burst into tears.

I don't remember much else. My mother put her arm around my shoulders and said something about it's not being anyone's fault. My father said something about going out for another ice-cream cake.

I saw Kristy lean over and whisper into Mary Anne's ear. I saw that Mary Anne looked as if she were close to crying herself (even then, Mary Anne was very, very sensitive).

"We'll go now," said Kristy suddenly.

" 'Bye . . ." I wailed, and ran out of the room.

"You still have presents to open." That was Janine, on the other side of my door. Everyone had been coming upstairs to be nice to me. And that just made it worse.

"Go away," I said. I was sulking in my room. I'd finished crying, but I hadn't finished feeling sorry for myself. I checked out my mournful self in the mirror, all dressed up in my birthday best with no birthday party to go to.

I could understand how kids might not have remembered their invitations, when I thought about it. After all, I had trouble remembering things in school for even a minute. I could understand if Mimi had forgotten to write the magic RSVP on some of the invitations. I could even understand, sort of, how everyone could miss my party.

But it still hurt. It was like when I had fallen skating and skinned my arm. I knew why I fell. But I still felt dumb. And my arm still hurt.

I heard the back door open and close as I moped on the bed, and figured my dad must have gone to his office, as he does some Saturdays. Probably Janine had gone to the library. She liked to go with my mom to the library in the summer and sit in the kids' reading room.

And wherever Mimi was, she'd probably just forgotten about my birthday by now, like everyone else. That's what I decided as I sprawled on the bed and stared up at the ceiling. I let tears leak out of the corners of my eyes and down my earlobes onto the pillow.

I decided I hated circuses. And birthdays.

A long time passed. I didn't know how long. But then I heard another knock at the door.

"Go away," I said angrily.

"My Claudia, it is me," said Mimi. "If you will please open the door, I have a request to make of you."

"Right now?" I asked, still sounding very grouchy.

"Yes, now," said Mimi firmly.

Reluctantly, slowly, I got up and opened the door. Mimi smiled when she saw me. I didn't smile back.

"You've been crying," said Mimi. "I would cry also. Then I would put cold water on my face so I would feel better." As she was talking, she took my hand and led me to the bathroom. She ran water on a facecloth and wiped my tear-streaked cheeks (and earlobes) with it.

"There," she said.

"Thank you," I replied. "May I go back to my room now?"

"In a minute. But first I need you to help me. I must go to Mary Anne's house."

"Why?" I asked.

Mimi didn't answer. She smoothed my jacket (I was still wearing my birthday lion tamer's outfit) and took my hand again.

"I don't see why you need me to go to Mary Anne's house with you," I complained.

Mimi smiled at me and led me across the street without answering. Instead of going to the front door, she led me around the side of the house.

"Mimi," I began. But I didn't get to finish. As Mimi opened the gate to the Spiers' backyard, what sounded like a hundred voices shouted, "SURPRISE!"

And then they began to sing "Happy Birthday."

I was shocked. I let go of Mimi's hand and stood there with my mouth open.

The Thomases, the Spiers, and my family were standing there, wearing silly party hats

Can you tell Im very surprised?

and big grins. The picnic table in the Spiers' backyard was draped with the circus cloth. Places had been set at the table and the pin the nose on the clown game had been thumbtacked to the gardening shed at the side of the yard. And there was an enormous homemade chocolate cake with lit candles — and the lion tamer in the middle from the ice-cream cake.

"Hurry up!" said Kristy, pointing to the cake. "Blow out your candles and make a wish!"

Mimi gave me a little push. "Happy birthday, my Claudia," she said.

I walked forward in a daze and blew out my candles. Everyone burst into cheers and Mary Anne put a silly party hat on me, too.

We ate ice cream and cake and drank punch. And then we played pin the nose on the clown (Kristy won) and circus Simon says. No one won that because we were laughing too hard at people roaring like lions and walking like elephants and scratching like monkeys in the circus. Then my father painted silly clown faces on all of us, even Mimi.

After that I opened my presents. My mouth fell open when I saw them piled up on the blanket under the tree. Then I realized that my family had brought their presents over. And Kristy and Mary Anne had wrapped gifts from the people in their families.

I remember every one of the other presents, too — the neat set of paints I got from Mimi, (my first *real* paints); the little gold ring with a tiny red stone in it from my mom and dad (it was a garnet, but it was red because my birthstone is a ruby); the artist's notepad I got from Mary Anne; the beginning reader mystery I got from Janine (it took me forever to read it, because I wasn't even reading yet, but that's how I got hooked on mysteries); socks with dogs on the cuffs that I got from Kristy; Sam's and Charlie's old train set; a set of colored markers from Mr. Spier.

Every single person had given me a gift, maybe not a brand-new gift, but a gift that was neat and cool and thoughtful. I still have some of the gifts, such as the ring, which is way too small for my finger. I wear it on a gold chain around my neck sometimes. I gave the train set to David Michael for his birthday not too long ago. I still have that first mystery book. . . .

And I have a videotape, too. My father videotaped the entire party. I've watched that tape many times since: my mom hopping on one leg in the circus Simon says; Mimi letting my dad paint a clown face on her; Mimi and Kristy and Mary Anne and me all together, grinning (in clown paint) at the camera; me blowing out the candles and opening the gifts.

That's how I can remember so many of the details. But I think I would remember them anyway. No. I *know* I would remember them.

Because I had a kid's worst nightmare: I had a birthday party and no one came.

And then I had the best birthday ever. Because it was a surprise and because the people I really loved were there.

It was and is my favorite birthday. I will never, ever forget it.

The Truth About the Tooth Fairy

I'm skipping first grade. I'm going strate to second grade. I was used to school now. I had it down. I wasn't a grate student and I had truble sitting still and paying atention. But I wasn't the wurst student in the wurld, either. Then in the midle of secund grade — TRUBLE!

Do you remember second grade? That's when losing your baby teeth seems to reach its peak. Every time I turned around, some kid in my class was losing her (or his) teeth. And of course, Kristy had managed to lose two at the same time, which she announced during her second-grade show and tell. Even Mary Anne had lost a tooth (she was in Kristy's class, too). Mary Anne didn't announce it at show and tell, but she did bring it to school to show Kristy and me. Walking to school one morning, we compared the three teeth.

I thought they were interesting-looking. So did Kristy. Mary Anne was sort of squeamish about them, but she was proud that she'd let her dad pull out her loose tooth without even crying.

I ran my tongue around the inside of my mouth. No loose teeth. "I'm not going to lose any of my teeth," I announced.

We had almost reached school. Janine had put her book in her backpack and she heard me.

"Of course you will," she said. "Everyone does. You lose your baby teeth so you can get your adult teeth."

"Yeah," said Kristy. "Besides, you get money or presents from the tooth fairy!"

"I hope I get enough money to buy that

jogging outfit for my Barbie doll," said Mary Anne. She giggled and I saw the gap where she'd lost her lower tooth. "If I don't get enough from this tooth, maybe the next one will do it."

"Ugh," I said, and walked into my classroom. I didn't look back as Kristy and Mary Anne hurried down the hall to their classroom. I didn't want to talk about this tooth fairy business anymore.

Because I knew the Truth about the tooth fairy.

The tooth fairy ate teeth. And not just teeth you left under your pillow to lure her into your room. Loose teeth, still inside your head. Like, if you were sleeping with your mouth open and the tooth fairy were around, she would just yank the tooth right out of your head.

And maybe some of your good teeth, too.

I don't know how I knew this. But I wasn't the only one who did. Emily Bernstein, who sat beside me, and Rick Chow, who sat in front of me, and I had been talking about it. Emily (who, like me, hadn't lost a tooth yet) said her mother and father wouldn't talk about the tooth fairy *at all*. We agreed that that was suspicious.

And Rick Chow, who had just lost his first tooth, had actually caught the tooth fairy in his room. He woke up one night to see a huge, dark shape bending over his bed. He closed his eyes and his mouth and stayed absolutely still.

This sounded terrifying to me. "Was your tooth missing when you woke up in the morning?"

"No," said Rick. "It was still just loose. But I knew the tooth fairy wanted to yank it out. That's why I shut my mouth!"

"Wow," said Emily. "Then what happened?"

"The tooth fairy said my name."

Emily and I shuddered.

"But I didn't answer. I knew not to open my mouth. So then she went away!"

"Wow," Emily said again. "No way am I letting the tooth fairy in *my* room."

"Me either," I said.

Of course we didn't tell anybody else about this. The other kids would not have believed us. Any more than we believed them when they talked about losing teeth and hiding them under their pillows while they were asleep and waiting for a visit from the tooth fairy who would leave them presents or money in exchange for their teeth.

Apart from the tooth fairy business, I really liked second grade. In fact, it was probably the last year I liked school. I was slow at reading and terrible at spelling — but lots of kids were still bad at spelling then. And Mr. Eccles, a tall, thin man, who wore jeans and a suit jacket and a little bow tie, didn't mind that I was easily distracted. "When you have trouble paying attention, Claudia," he told me, "ask a question." He didn't mind when I'd suddenly blurt questions out in the middle of reading or arithmetic.

And Mr. Eccles made learning new things fun. We didn't just read about them, we learned *all* about them. Mr. Eccles was a cool teacher.

For instance, when Cokie Mason was the first person to lose a tooth during school (and of course bragged about it in show and tell as if we were all a bunch of big babies who hadn't lost any of our own teeth yet), Mr. Eccles said that different people lose teeth at different times, and then he started talking about how sharks lose hundreds and hundreds of teeth (which made Cokie turn green and made the rest of us laugh).

Then Mr. Eccles said that we'd study teeth, and we did. Only it hadn't been some boring "All About Your Teeth" unit like poor Mary Anne and Kristy had in *their* second-grade class.

Instead we'd studied the teeth of different kinds of animals and what they're used for, and Mr. Eccles had brought in a shark's tooth from a family summer fishing expedition on a charter boat. The captain of the charter boat had given it to him and we'd been fascinated by it.

We'd learned that meat-eaters have different teeth than grass-eaters. We learned about calcium, which makes your teeth strong, and about the ways you can get calcium besides milk. (We'd even learned that there are whole cultures that never drink milk!)

All in all, it had been a pretty cool unit. We'd even had a dentist come visit our class. She had brought along a big set of plastic teeth and told us funny stories about being a dentist. And that day, the art teacher was coming in to help Mr. Eccles and our class make papier-mâché models of teeth. Our group (Rick and Emily and me) already knew what we were going to make: a walrus tusk.

First we looked up walruses and read about them. Emily read aloud and Rick took notes. Then we had to figure out what size tusk we wanted to make (that was easy — life-sized). Then we had to measure out how much of each ingredient we needed to make our papier-mâché. After that we went to work.

We added a little tiny bit of brown watercolor paint to our papier-mâché because the picture in the book showed that walrus tusks weren't white but ivory-colored.

"Excellent, excellent," said Mr. Eccles. "It's a good thing there are no walruses around. They'd think you'd stolen their tusk!"

We thought that was hugely funny, of course. When we finished, we put our tusk on the bookshelf by the window to dry.

I was very proud of that tusk.

But it made me a little uneasy, too. Because I'd somehow added the tusk to my mental picture of the tooth fairy. I shuddered at the image: something big and dark and hairy with enormous tusk teeth sticking out of its face. I imagined it leaning over my bed. I imagined it whispering "Claudia, Claudiaaaaaaaaa."

I clamped my mouth shut just thinking about it.

Yes, I knew the Truth about the tooth fairy. And I didn't want the hairy fairy anywhere near me or my teeth, no matter what Kristy or Mary Anne or any of my friends said.

But it had to happen. I had to start losing my teeth. Although I started brushing them three and even four times a day to make them stay healthy and last a long, long time, I finally got my first loose tooth.

By accident.

We were playing tag on the playground at afternoon recess. I was running at top speed, looking over my shoulder. Suddenly Kristy called, "Claudia, look out!"

But it was too late. I crashed into Pete Black and we fell over in a heap. I hit my mouth on the ground.

"OWWW!" I cried as Pete scrambled to his feet. I raised my hand to my mouth. Was it bleeding? Or worse, had I knocked out a tooth?

"Are you all right, Claudia?" asked Mr. Eccles.

I lowered my hand. No blood. No tooth. I ran my tongue around my mouth just to make sure. All my teeth were still there. "Yes," I said, embarrassed that I had fallen.

Mr. Eccles bent down to inspect my face. "You've got a scrape on your lip," he pointed out.

"It doesn't hurt," I said quickly. I didn't want to go to the nurse's office where she might put something on it that would hurt worse.

Mr. Eccles inspected my lip for a moment longer, then nodded. "Okay," he said.

"Good," said Emily, who'd been chasing me. She slapped me on the shoulder. "Then you're it!"

Everyone took off and I took off, too. I forgot about my fall. Sort of.

But by the end of the day, as I was walking home with Kristy and Mary Anne, my mouth had started to hurt. No. Not my mouth. My front tooth.

In fact, it had started to throb. And when I talked, it hurt even more. So I kept quiet. Fortunately, Kristy and Mary Anne didn't seem to notice.

I was still safe from the hairy fairy.

Mimi noticed my scraped mouth the moment I walked in the door. "What happened, my Claudia?" she asked.

"I fell playing tag," I said, keeping my answer short because it hurt to move my mouth.

Janine sat down at the kitchen table and began eating an apple. As she bit in with her front teeth, I winced.

"Would you like an apple?" asked Mimi.

"No," I said. "Thanks."

"You are not hungry?" Mimi looked surprised. I was always hungry when I got home from school. Maybe not for an apple, but for something.

I didn't wait around to see if I could get cookies or popcorn instead. I just said, "I'm not hungry," and made my escape upstairs to my room.

I started my homework. But it was hard to concentrate when my tooth hurt. I sneaked out a mystery book and tried to read that. It was one I'd read before, one of my favorites. But it didn't hold my attention now.

And I couldn't eat any of the gooey, excellent snacks hidden in my room. My tooth wouldn't take it.

Of course, I couldn't go around with my mouth shut forever, hairy fairy or not. That night at dinner, my parents got the truth out of me the moment I asked if I could be excused from dinner.

"But you had nothing to eat when you returned home from school today," said Mimi.

My father put his hand on my forehead. "Are you coming down with something?"

"What happened to your mouth?" my mother asked.

"I fell at school today playing tag."

My father touched my upper lip. I couldn't help it. "Ow!" I cried.

"Hold still," he said. He gently lifted my upper lip.

"Orrw," I mumbled. "On't touch y tooth."

"You hit your tooth when you fell," said my mother. "Oh, Claudia. I bet that hurt."

My father let go of my lip. He patted me on the shoulder. "Looks like you're about to lose your first tooth," he said, smiling.

"No! It's not even loose!"

"I think we'd better go to the dentist tomorrow," said my mom.

"I'll get you something soft to eat that will not hurt your tooth," said Mimi.

"It's fine, it's fine," I cried. But it was too late. My fate was sealed.

I was *not* happy in school the next day. I had to go to the dentist. Dr. Rice was our family's dentist. I had been to visit him, just for a check-up, and hadn't minded at all. But what if he wanted to pull my tooth? Then the hairy tooth fairy would get me.

At Dr. Rice's, when he said, "Open wide, Claudia," I closed my eyes and my mouth and slid down into the chair.

"Claudia," said Dr. Rice. I opened my eyes just a little. Dr. Rice was smiling a puzzled smile. I felt silly.

"It doesn't hurt," I said.

"What doesn't hurt?" asked Dr. Rice. "Why don't you show me?"

I opened my mouth and pointed to my front tooth. "I fell. But it doesn't hurt. Not *really*."

Dr. Rice looked at my tooth. "Hmmm," he said. He tapped the tooth with his metal tooth gadget, very gently.

"Owww," I said. Then I said, "Maybe it hurts a little."

Dr. Rice took an X ray of my tooth. When the X ray came back he held it up and showed me the picture of my tooth. That was pretty interesting. The dentist who had visited our class had showed us X-rays of teeth, too. But it was more interesting looking at X rays of my own teeth.

Then Dr. Rice said, "Claudia, there's a tooth right behind your front tooth. It may not be quite ready to come in, but it will be ready soon. And your front baby tooth needs to come out. I'm going to send you to Dr. Celenza. She specializes in things like pulling teeth."

For a moment I imagined Dr. Celenza holding a pair of big pliers and pulling out the hairy tooth fairy's tusks. That almost made me smile.

But then I thought about having my own tooth pulled. That definitely did *not* make me smile.

Meanwhile, Dr. Rice was telling my mother about Dr. Celenza and my tooth.

I was going to have my tooth pulled out the very next morning. I wasn't even going to go to school first. That idea cheered me up a little. But not much.

I remember having "tooth" food for dinner that night: soup and mashed potatoes and milk, and for dessert, a Ben & Jerry's Cherry Garcia milkshake. Everybody else had their ice cream in a bowl, but Mimi put mine through the blender and I drank it with a straw.

I would've enjoyed it if I hadn't been worried about 1) losing my tooth and whether that would hurt; and 2) the tooth fairy. They were about equal in my mind. After all, I believed that the tooth fairy was a sort of demented dentist who flew through the night yanking teeth out of the mouths of unsuspecting children.

By the time I reached Dr. Celenza's office, hanging onto both my mother's *and* Mimi's hands (I'd insisted that Mimi go with us) I was halfway convinced that Dr. Celenza and the wicked, tooth-yanking tooth fairy were one and the same. So I was surprised (and amazed) to see that her office didn't look like a real doctor's office. The walls were covered with colored stars of red, green, yellow, and blue. A silver moon hung from the ceiling. All around, looking out from behind stars or inside some of the stars, were pictures of smiling kids.

And the chair looked like a rocketship. The doctor's assistant helped me climb in the chair and showed me the make-believe control panel. I was so busy pushing the buttons and staring around the room that I didn't even notice Dr. Celenza come in until she was standing right beside me.

"Hi, Claudia," she said. "I'm Dr. Celenza." She had a friendly smile and was wearing lots of buttons on her white doctor's coat. The buttons said things like, "Tell the Tooth!" and had pictures of teeth on them. I would have thought they were funny if I hadn't been so worried.

"My tooth doesn't need to be pulled," I said.

"Hmm," said Dr. Celenza. "Why don't you let me take a look at it, since you're already here?"

"Well, okay," I said reluctantly. "But don't touch it."

I let Dr. Celenza look at my teeth. "You have good, healthy teeth, Claudia," she said. "But I need to touch your tooth. I know that might hurt. So I'm going to give you a quick shot of Novocain to put it to sleep so it won't hurt when I look at it."

That's what she did. The shot stung for a moment. Then my tooth stopped hurting.

"Can you feel that?" asked Dr. Celenza after a minute.

"Eel at?" I asked (my mouth was still open).

"Good," said Dr. Celenza. "You know what, I think that tooth really should come out, Claudia. And now that it's asleep, you won't feel anything."

I was about to object. I wasn't afraid of it hurting anymore — and I didn't think Dr. Celenza and the tooth fairy were in league together to get all my teeth. But having my tooth pulled meant that I'd have to let the tooth fairy into my room . . . unless . . . unless Dr. Celenza kept the tooth. And if she did, the tooth fairy would have to stay away!

I took a deep breath. "Okay," I said.

It was over in no time. Dr. Celenza congratulated me on "making the right decision" to have my tooth pulled, and she let me choose a prize for "being such a smart, good patient." The prizes were all jumbled up in a space helmet. I chose a packet of stick-on earrings. Dr. Celenza let me put the earrings on and I looked in the mirror and grinned. When I saw the gap where my tooth had been, I laughed. The earrings, little red apples, looked cool. But my tooth gap looked funny.

"You can eat real apples in a few days," Dr. Celenza told me. "Don't worry. But for the first couple of days, take it easy on your teeth."

"Okay," I said happily. I jumped out of the chair and hurried out to the waiting room. While Mom talked to Dr. Celenza, I showed Mimi my new stick-on earrings and described

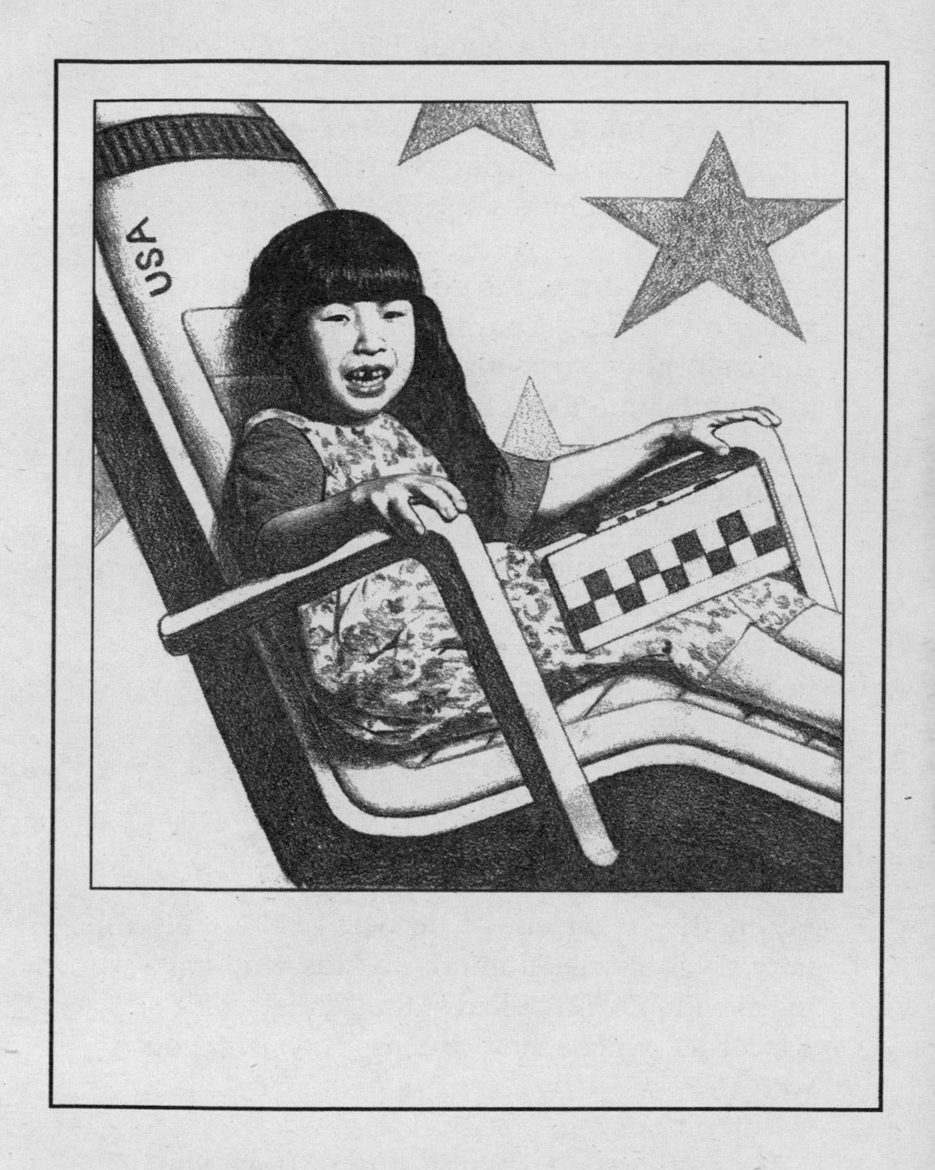

Who took my tooth? Dr. C. takes a Polaroid of all her pashunce -- cool, huh?

how brave I'd been about having my tooth pulled.

We were almost out the door and I had forgotten all my worries about the hairy t.f. when a voice behind us said, "Oh, my goodness! Wait!"

I turned and saw the doctor's assistant hurrying toward us. "Your tooth," he said. "You almost forgot your tooth! You want something to leave for the tooth fairy, don't you?"

I froze. My mother laughed and said, "Thank you." She took the vial with my tooth in it from the assistant and said to me, "What do you say, Claudia?"

"Thank you," I said reluctantly.

"Dr. Celenza said you were a terrific patient," my mother told me on the way home.

"You were very brave," Mimi added.

"I guess so," I said listlessly.

Neither my mother nor my grandmother seemed to notice. "You know what, Claudia?" my mother went on. "I do believe the tooth fairy gives special attention to kids who have to have their teeth pulled at the dentist's office. Especially when they are as brave as you were."

I didn't answer.

My mother said, "So be sure to leave your tooth under your pillow tonight."

"I will remind you," said Mimi, patting my hand.

I didn't answer. I kept my mouth closed. I was practicing for the arrival of the tooth fairy. I might have lost one tooth that day. But no way was I going to lose all the rest.

"You did not forget to put your tooth under your pillow?" asked Mimi. She'd come in to tell me good night, just as she did every night.

"No," I said. I lifted the pillow to show her.

She nodded and smiled. "Good night, my Claudia," she said and touched my forehead. Then she turned off the light on my bedside table and left the room.

The moment she was gone, I leaped up. I emptied out my piggy bank and lined the coins up along my windowsill so that if the t.f. tried to get in, she would knock the money over. I would hear the coins and have time to jump up and fight. (Also, there was always a chance that the tooth fairy would see all the money and just take that and leave.)

Then I closed the curtains and pulled the bottoms of them onto my desk (which was under the window). I put a stack of books on the curtains. Even if the t.f. was able to get past the money trap, she would have to open the curtains. When she did, *ka-bam!* The books would fall over and wake me up.

I put Vaseline on the window latch (which would make it harder to open). Then I took my clothes and bunched them into a dummy figure under the blankets and covered it up. Even if the t.f. was able to get past all my traps, she wouldn't find me there. I wasn't going to be caught. I was going to hide in the closet until I was sure I was safe.

I took one of the pillows into the closet with me and propped it against the wall. Then I piled my shoes around me. I was going to use them for ammunition to throw at the tooth fairy, if necessary.

I had my flashlight with me and, for a while, I tried to read. But every little sound made me jump, and I worried the t.f. would see the light coming from the closet (if she made it past all my traps) and would come after me and my remaining teeth.

It was hard staying awake. The closet was uncomfortable, but in spite of that, my eyes kept drooping. Then a sound would startle me momentarily awake. They were just the normal sounds of my house, though.

Gradually, the house grew quiet. And dark. And still.

And then I heard it. A sound.

Someone was coming into my room.

Cautiously I peered around the closet door. My eyes widened. A tiny square of light from the hall was coming into my room through my bedroom door. I recognized my mother.

Before I could think what to do, my mother tiptoed over to my bed. "Claudia?" she said softly.

Of course, I didn't answer.

It was very dark but I was sure I saw mother slide her hand carefully under my pillow and take something out from under it. Then she slid something else back under the pillow and tiptoed carefully from the room, closing the door softly behind her.

I pushed the door open and leaped across the room. I turned on my flashlight and lifted the pillow.

My tooth was gone. In its place was a shiny Susan B. Anthony dollar.

I looked over my shoulder. I guess I was confused and still expected the tooth fairy to come swooping in through the window. But nothing happened.

And then I realized why.

My mother was the tooth fairy. There was no real tooth fairy.

I'd never been so relieved in my life. I could lose the rest of my baby teeth safely. No one was going to come sneaking in my room and pull them out when I wasn't looking. Nothing huge and hairy was going to lean over my bed and whisper my name.

I was safe. No t.f.

I put my clothes back in the closet and dismantled my traps. I dropped my money back in my piggy bank — except for my dollar. I left that under my pillow. When I'd gotten back in bed and laid down, I slid my hand under the pillow and felt the rough edges and smooth cool metal. A whole dollar for my tooth. Not bad. Wait till I told Mary Anne and Kristy.

And wait till I told them what I'd figured out. . . .

I was almost asleep, clutching my dollar, when another thought made my eyelids fly open. I sat straight up in bed.

"The Easter Bunny!" I gasped. "Santa Claus!"

Was it possible? Could it be true? It had to be.

If the tooth fairy wasn't real, then neither was the Easter Bunny or Santa. My parents were the ones who hid the Easter eggs in our backyard every year and ate the carrot I left out. My parents were the ones who filled the stockings Janine and I hung from the chimney and left the presents by the tree for us to open on Christmas morning.

No giant rabbit (with giant rabbit teeth) had ever hopped into our yard to hide eggs and fill up the Easter baskets we left on the back steps next to the plate.

No fat jolly man with eight tiny reindeer had ever landed on our roof. No big guy dressed in red had stopped to nibble on the cookies and drink the glass of milk we'd left on the mantle.

No Easter Bunny. No Santa Claus.

It had to be true. Slowly I lay down again, staring up into the darkness, thinking hard. Was I relieved? Or was I sad?

I wasn't sure. But I felt different. I felt that I wasn't a kid anymore. I felt grown-up.

Later, I would ask my parents and they would tell me the truth, the whole truth, and nothing but about the tooth fairy and company. Later, I would tell Kristy and Mary Anne what I had believed about the tooth fairy and we would all laugh.

For the moment, however, I wasn't sure what to think.

But it was a big moment in my life. A milestone. I knew I would never forget it.

Boo for Fourth Grade

after my discovurey about the tooth fairy, and all the rest, second grade was a piece of cake Realy. I wasn't the best student in the class, but I wasn't the wurst. And Mr. Eccles was my favorit person in the whole world (beside my friends and family, of course). Third grade, tho, wasnt so neat. And forth grade ... well, this is the first tim Ive ever talked about this. Only Kristy and Mary Anne realy know about it. And I made them promis not to talk about it, it was so terible...

Boo for Fourth Grade

My third-grade teacher wasn't bad, but she wasn't great. Mrs. Colquiet, I realize now, just didn't have much of an imagination. She followed Plans. She followed Rules. She wore Business Suits. (I think that says it all.)

That was hard for me, especially after Mr. Eccles.

It was also hard because Janine had had Mrs. Colquiet and she had been Mrs. Colquiet's best student. The very first thing Mrs. Colquiet said to me on the very first day of third grade was, "Claudia Kishi? Janine Kishi's younger sister?"

I nodded miserably. I knew what was coming. And it did. Mrs. Colquiet's face broke into a huge smile. "Janine Kishi. An outstanding student. Your family must be very, very proud of her."

"Yes," I said.

"Well, well, well . . ." Mrs. Colquiet gave me another beaming smile and kept on calling roll.

For a little while — until she found out how different I was from Janine — I was her favorite student.

Then I began to fall further and further behind. And not just because of Mrs. Colquiet, who, to be fair, never, ever compared me to Janine. But I *felt* as if she were comparing us, which made it even worse when I would get spelling tests back and the big red number at the top would be the lowest grade in the class. And although spelling wasn't my worst subject, I often made the worst grades on the spelling tests. I made major errors on my math homework. I got whole countries mixed up in geography.

You get the idea.

But because I hadn't done so badly with Mr. Eccles, I just figured it wasn't so important. And I think my parents figured part of it was that I didn't do as well with Mrs. Colquiet's style of teaching. Mrs. Colquiet wasn't terrible. In fact, she was very careful to tell my parents, even on my worst report cards, that my talent for art made me the best artist in the class.

I started fourth grade thinking things would be better, especially when I learned that Kristy was in my class. I hadn't been in a class with Kristy since first grade.

"Guess what?" Kristy told me on the morning of the first day of school.

"What?" I said.

"We got Ms. Jameson," said Kristy. "She's really cool. She's from the south and she has this neat accent and she does cool stuff." Kristy nodded for emphasis. "Charlie had her. He told me all about her."

"Good," I said. I was ready to like Ms. Jameson. And I did, the moment she walked into the room. She was dressed casually, the way Mr. Eccles used to dress — in jeans and a jacket and she even had on a sort of tie. Her black hair was cut short and close to her head, and she was wearing gold hoop earrings. She had dark brown skin and dark brown eyes and a soft voice with a real southern accent. I'd never heard a southern accent before, except on television, and I was fascinated.

She spoke softly, too. At first I thought the class would just roll right over her, everybody talking at the top of their lungs. But we didn't. Something about the way she spoke, and then looked at us, as if she were talking one grown-up to another, made us settle down.

Soon the classroom was so quiet, you could practically hear a pin (or maybe I mean a pen) drop.

Ms. Jameson nodded, and welcomed us to her classroom. "But it's not just my classroom," she told us. "It's your classroom, too. We're all responsible for what we learn here. There's a saying my grandmother taught me: it takes a village to raise a child. We are, in a sense, a village. We are part of it. It takes all of us to make sure each of us is the best that she or he can be."

I didn't understand everything she was saying, but I liked the sound of it. And I liked

Ms. Jameson. I especially liked her when I found out she had had Janine as a student, too. I found out because Janine told me. Ms. Jameson never mentioned it.

Ms. Jameson became my new favorite teacher of all time — or at least, she tied with Mr. Eccles.

What I didn't like was the schoolwork.

Somehow, between second and fourth grade, I'd gotten lost. I didn't understand anything anymore.

"I *hate* school!" I told Mimi one afternoon, slamming my spelling book closed.

Mimi looked shocked. I had never done that before. But I was tired of the way my spelling words were never spelled the way they sounded. I didn't understand it.

"I don't need to be able to spell, anyway," I said. "I'm going to be an *artist*. Artists don't have to spell."

"But even artists must go to school," Mimi reminded me. She picked up the book and pulled it toward her. "Let us practice the words one more time. I think you are getting better."

I didn't think I was. In fact, I knew I wasn't. But I kept trying.

I tried for my mom, who brought special books home from the library and worked with me at the kitchen table at night.

I tried for my dad, who explained math and science to me, reading ahead in my books so he could understand enough to show me what I was supposed to be learning.

I tried for Mimi, always.

I even tried for Janine, who wanted to help me with my book reports. But Janine didn't understand what it was like not to understand. If it took a village to raise a child, Janine would have been the village genius.

And I would have been the village dummy.

Ms. Jameson tried to help me, too, of course. She never wrote my grades in big, mean red letters. She didn't believe in announcing grades in class. She let me do some of my book reports orally, with illustrations instead of in writing.

But it wasn't enough. Finally, one day, she sent a note home with my parents — along with the worst report card I'd ever gotten.

"You are a bright girl," Ms. Jameson said to me. "You are without question one of the most creative students and one of the most imaginative I have ever had in my class. But you are not achieving up to your level of intelligence . . ."

"Underachiever," I muttered. I'd heard the word before. I hated it. In my mind it meant "dumb kid who doesn't try." But I did try.

Ms. Jameson surprised me. She took my

hand and said, "Perhaps that is not the best word. You achieve great things in some areas." She put the note in my hand and closed my fingers around it. "Give this to your parents, and I will talk to them."

A parent-teacher conference. Well, I'd been the subject of those before. That was nothing new. At least, that's what I kept telling myself as I walked home from school with Mary Anne and Kristy.

We didn't discuss our report cards. We never did. Kristy and Mary Anne made good grades and I didn't, and we'd just stopped talking about the report cards somewhere in the middle of third grade.

My family always talked about them at home, though. But not this one. That was almost worse than anything. My mother looked at my report card and then she said, "Oh, Claudia."

"I tried," I said. "I really did."

"I think you did," said my mom. "I do." And then she didn't say anything else to me about it. She must have called my father before he left the office, because he didn't say anything, either. Then, two days later, they went to school to talk to Ms. Jameson on my mother's day off from the library.

When I got home from school that day, Mom was waiting for me.

That scared me. "I'm not expelled, am I?" I cried before I even put my books down.

"Claudia, of course not!" My mother looked indignant. "But we are thinking of trying . . . Ms. Jameson suggested a couple of approaches. A test for learning disabilities . . ." My mom's voice trailed off. She frowned, then tried to look more cheerful. "Or a school more suited to someone who has your particular talents, talents that are visual, rather than verbal or mathematical."

"Another school! But Mom, all my friends are at Stoneybrook Elementary! I don't want to go to another school."

My mother pulled me closer to her and smoothed back my bangs. "It's just one possibility, Claudia. There's a private school in Stamford that Ms. Jameson particularly recommended. Of course, there are tests you have to take to get in. . . ."

The moment I heard the word "tests" I stopped worrying. There was no way I would ever pass any entrance test to any school. And even though I tried as hard as I could to pass every test at SES, I resolved immediately that I would try to do just the opposite on any entrance exam to any private school.

My mother had been watching me anxiously. She looked *very* relieved when I nodded.

I shrugged. "Oh, okay," I said.

"It's nothing definite," Mom went on. "But I wouldn't feel right if we didn't check into it, particularly after Ms. Jameson recommended it."

I had thought Ms. Jameson liked me. But maybe she didn't after all. That hurt.

I resolved to try harder. I even tried to convince my parents that it wouldn't be good for me to have to skip school to go all the way to Stamford to be interviewed for the Stamford Alternative Academy, and to take their tests. My parents disagreed. So on the very last day of November, we drove to Stamford.

The academy was pretty: lots of rolling grounds and low buildings with big trees. The gym, standing on one corner of a lawn, was awesome. Inside the administration building, my mother pointed to the student artwork on the wall.

I tried to be polite, but personally I thought SES was much better. Not so fancy. Not so formal. Not so stuck-up.

I was polite in the interviews, but I tried not to tell them too much about myself — except when they asked me how I saw myself as a student.

"Oh, I'm a *terrible* student," I told the two women who were interviewing me (I had three interviews in all, plus the tests). "Terrible, and

Stamford Alternative Academy

SAA

Stamford, Connecticut

nice place to visit, but I did'nt want to go to school here!

I'm getting worse all the time. *Everyone* says I'm an underachiever, and I guess maybe they're right."

There. That should convince them that they didn't want me at their academy. The two women looked solemn and made notes on their yellow pads. Then they asked me what my strengths were.

I thought a moment, then said, "Oh, I don't really think I have *any*. Sometimes teachers say I'm good in art, but you know what I think? I think they're saying that because I'm so terrible at everything else."

The two interviewers looked even more solemn and made a lot more notes without speaking.

When the interview was over, I left feeling more cheerful. For once it had felt good to say I was a terrible student. And even though I knew I was a good artist and getting better all the time, I hadn't minded telling that fib about what my teachers said. And who knows — maybe it had been true for my third-grade teacher, so it wasn't a complete fib after all.

I was in a good mood on the way home. I had skipped a whole day of SES, and I had passed the tests at SAA with flying colors, at least the way I saw it. I was pretty sure I'd failed them all.

Good-bye, Stamford Alternative Academy.

So you can imagine how shocked I was the week before Thanksgiving when my parents gave me the news after dinner one night.

I'd been accepted at Stamford Alternative Academy. I was going to begin school the second semester of the year, after Christmas vacation.

"You're kidding!" I gasped.

"Isn't it wonderful?" said my mother. "The classes are very small. And students are put into classes according to their level. The emphasis is not on competition and comparison with other children, but on working at your own pace."

"Plus lots of help and individual attention," my father said.

"I don't *want* help and individual attention," I replied, trying to gather my stunned wits. "You and Mom and Mimi — and, and Janine — give me plenty of that! Besides, how can you trust that school? Did they tell you I passed all those entrance tests to get in? I didn't, I know I didn't!"

My father looked puzzled. "Those weren't entrance tests," he said. "Those are given only to determine your strengths and weaknesses. You were accepted on the basis of your remedial needs. The school thinks it can help you."

"No! No! I won't go!" I cried, and ran out of the room.

But I didn't have a choice. My parents let me sulk and complain for a few days. Then they sat me down for another talk. And they made it clear that nothing I could say or do would change their minds. I was going to Stamford Alternative Academy at the beginning of the second semester.

The rest of my time at SES was a nightmare. People made plans for Christmas and I felt left out. Kristy and Mary Anne complained about walking to school in the cold. Mary Anne was hoping her father would let her get a new, less babyish coat for Christmas. "I think he's weakening," she said. "He actually said he liked the color of your parka the other day, Claudia."

I tried to be enthusiastic. I managed to make myself act reasonably normal. But inside I felt numb. And too embarrassed to tell my friends about transferring to a "special" school. I didn't think they wouldn't be my friends because of it, but I knew they'd be walking to school every morning without me. They'd be doing things at SES without me. Soon I would be forgotten.

Soon I'd be all alone at the "special" school.

On the last day of school before winter vacation, Ms. Jameson kept me after class for a moment. I'd been sneaking all my stuff home a little at a time so that I didn't have to clean out my desk or my locker.

"I've enjoyed having you as a student, Claudia," she said.

"My friends are waiting," I replied.

"Good luck," said Ms. Jameson.

"Good-bye," I said. "And thanks." Under my breath as I walked out, I added, "For nothing."

If Ms. Jameson had really liked having me as a student, why had she recommended I be exiled to Stamford?

Phooey on Ms. Jameson.

I don't remember much about Christmas that year. It just sort of floated by. I finally got up the nerve to tell Kristy and Mary Anne that I wouldn't be going back to SES — the night before I started at Stamford. (SAA started a day earlier than SES.)

They were totally shocked. And totally supportive. They told me not to worry. That we'd always be friends. That it would probably be cool. They teased me about how lucky I was not to have to walk to school (my father was going to drive me to SAA on his way to work).

It didn't help. It made me feel worse than ever.

The morning I left for SAA, the sky was

gray and a few soggy, fat, ugly flakes of snow were starting to fall. I sat in the corner of the front seat as far from my father as I could get. He kept up a cheerful conversation on the way. I stuck to "yes" and "no." He pretended he didn't notice.

When we reached the school, I thought for a moment about pretending to climb the front steps and then running away the moment my father left. But I didn't get a chance. A tall, thin woman with a friendly smile opened the door at the top of the steps and waved. "You must be Claudia Kishi!" she called.

"What is she, my baby-sitter?" I asked my father. He gave me the look that said I had gone too far.

" 'Bye," I said quickly and got out of the car. I walked up the stairs as slowly as I dared. I didn't look back. I didn't look up as the tall woman put her hand on my shoulder and said, "I'm Corla Magnusson, the academic coordinator. Welcome to Stamford Alternative Academy."

My life was over.

Kristy and Mary Anne came over to my house the moment I returned home from my first day at Stamford Alternative Academy. I told them how much I hated it. Kristy said I should just try to flunk out. She didn't believe it when I told her I had already tried . . . and failed.

That was the thing about the SAA. It *looked* like a normal school, except maybe prettier and neater, more picture bookish. But at SAA, they didn't believe in failure. No one ever even said the word. If you didn't get something right, they said things such as, "Hmmm. Well, what about trying it this way?"

The classes were small, too. Tiny. So if I was having a problem with spelling or math or I stopped paying attention for even an instant, a teacher would suddenly be there, bending over and saying, "How's it going, Claudia?"

"Crummy!" I wanted to shout. "Horrible!"

But if I had, I wouldn't have been telling the whole truth. Because one thing wasn't crummy and horrible anymore — my schoolwork.

I began to get an idea of what was going on in math. I learned how to look at the way things were written so I could understand the contents, and remember what I'd read more easily. And because there weren't a bunch of other kids with big fat A+s and 100s written on the tops of their papers (SAA, remember, didn't believe in that kind of grading), I didn't feel stupid when it took me a long time to figure something out. The important thing was that I did figure it out. And when I did, my answer was just as good and just as right as anybody else's.

Too bad I didn't have any friends to share it with.

I didn't have any friends at SAA because I didn't want any. Oh, the kids weren't weird or anything like that, although I guess I'd expected them to be. I mean, no matter how you said it, SAA was a school for kids who didn't do well in school. Which to my way of thinking meant the kids would be weird.

But I was wrong about that. If anything, I was one of the weirder kids in the school. I liked to wear bright colors and I was already making my own jewelry and sewing different kinds of buttons on my shirts. Most of the other kids dressed more like kids in Gap ads.

The girl who sat next to me, in Core Group (that's what our main class was called), had said hello the very first day after I'd been walked to my class by Ms. Magnusson. She was short with neat, shoulder-length brown hair and friendly blue eyes.

"I'm Mary Rose," she said, giving me a big smile. "You've got a good Core. Mr. Ho, our Core teacher, is neat."

"I'm so excited," I said sarcastically.

Mary Rose had looked surprised and then hurt. "Well," she finally said, "let me know if you need any help."

Unfortunate choice of words. Wasn't I at SAA because everybody said I needed help? But who wants help if they haven't asked for it?

"I *don't* need any help. *Thank* you," I said.

Mary Rose hadn't spoken to me since. And I hadn't bothered to talk to anybody else. I even ate lunch alone, which of course made me feel sorrier for myself than ever.

My days were all boringly the same now: get up, get dressed, leave earlier than ever because my father had to drive me to Stamford on his way to work. Since I arrived at school a little early, I went to the Open Area. It was

Doing time at SAA. A photo that didn't make the yeerbook.

part of the school library, a big, sunny room off to one side with long tables where you could sit and study or read or even play quiet games with other students.

I drew sketches in my notebook. Or I sat and stared out of the window until the first bell rang.

At the sound of the first bell, we all went to Core Group. When I wasn't in Core Group I was in language arts or art class.

I actually enjoyed art class. It was the only good part of the day: a whole period, every single day, to work on art projects. And I could do anything I wanted. It was a small class like all the others, but in this class no teacher swooped down every time I stopped and stared off into space. The art teacher understood that creating things takes time — without interruptions.

At the end of the day, I stood on the steps with the other kids, waiting for my mother or father to show up. When one of them did, I walked down the steps and got in the car without saying anything to anybody. It was the end of another long, quiet, mostly boring, horrible day.

My parents always said, with big smiles, "How was your day, Claudia?"

"Fine," I would say in a tone of voice that meant just the opposite. They always ignored my tone of voice. After awhile I just stopped answering and shrugged.

It didn't help that I hardly ever got to see Kristy and Mary Anne anymore. Not only did I not talk to anyone at my dumb new school, but because the dumb new school was in Stamford, I was always late getting home. Usually Kristy and Mary Anne had already walked home from school (together) and had started their homework or were doing something else (together) by the time I returned home. At first, if they were hanging out, I would join them. But after awhile I realized that I was always the one going over to Kristy's house (and, less often, to Mary Anne's, because she had all these weird baby-sitters her father kept hiring to stay after school with her until he got home). They never came over to my house.

Plus my life wasn't the same as theirs anymore. For instance, there was the new language arts project that all the fourth-grade classes at SES were working on: each class was writing a play based on a book chosen by the class. Then they were going to rehearse a scene and present it at a special fourth-grade assembly.

"Or it might be a whole school assembly," Kristy said when I was at her house late one afternoon.

"You should do Nancy Drew," I said instantly.

"We are going to have a class vote," Kristy told me. "We each wrote down a favorite book and then Ms. Jameson is making a list of them and we're going to vote on them. The book that gets the most votes, wins."

"I would have written down Nancy Drew," I said.

"I think my class is going to do *The Wizard of Oz*," said Mary Anne.

"You'd make a great Dorothy," I said. I meant it, too. With her bangs and braids, Mary Anne would have looked just like Dorothy.

"I want to do *Harriet the Spy*," said Kristy. "And be Harriet."

"I could never be *in* the play," said Mary Anne.

"You could be a director or writer or costume designer," said Kristy. "Or make the scenery."

Costume designer. Making scenery. Right away, I could think of a million ideas. Those were things I could have done, if I'd still been a part of my class. If Ms. Jameson hadn't betrayed me. If my parents hadn't made me go to another school.

I listened to Kristy and Mary Anne talking. The project sounded like so much fun. But it didn't matter. I wasn't a part of all that anymore.

A little while later, I left. Mary Anne and Kristy were still talking excitedly about the play. They didn't notice that I hadn't had a thing to say.

I didn't go to Kristy's again for a couple of days. I admit, it was sort of a test to see if they'd even noticed I was gone.

They did. Kristy called me on the third afternoon the moment I walked in the door (she must have been watching my house from hers).

"Where've you been?" she demanded when I answered. She didn't even say hello.

"Kristy?" I asked, pretending to be surprised.

"You know it's me," she said. "Where have you been?"

"At school. With no one to talk to. Ever. Then I come home. And sometimes I talk to Mimi. Or even Janine, if she's not studying."

"Why don't you come over? Now," said Kristy. "Mary Anne's coming over in a little while, too."

"Why don't you come over here?" I burst out. "Why don't you and Mary Anne ever come over here anymore?"

"We do," said Kristy.

"You don't."

"We . . ." Her voice trailed off. "Oh. I guess we haven't. Gosh, Claudia, it's just 'cause we walk home from school together and plan to go to my house — or Mary Anne's, when she doesn't have some goofy baby-sitter."

I sighed. I knew it was true. I knew that my friends weren't forgetting about me on purpose.

"Can we come over today?"

"Yes," I said.

Not too much later, Kristy and Mary Anne came to my house. We decided to make chocolate chip cookies. It was fun. We laughed and giggled and added weird flavorings to the cookies and then we sat around and ate them. Kristy told a funny story about Louie stealing a loaf of bread that her mother had just opened and put on the kitchen table. He'd run through the house shaking the bag and scattering slices of bread everywhere and then run back through it, trying to eat them as he ran (and to keep from being caught).

"Did he get in trouble?" asked Mary Anne, her eyes round.

"Not really," said Kristy. "Louie's a dog and Mom said dogs make mistakes. She said it's the same as if a two-year-old pulled the bread off the table. A two-year-old doesn't know that's wrong and neither did Louie, until she told him. And he thought we were playing a game when we were chasing him. Mom said next time she'll know not to put the bread on the table when Louie's sitting right there watching every move she makes."

We laughed. Then Mary Anne sighed. "I wish my father would let me get a pet."

We talked about that and for awhile I forgot how out-of-things I felt. But inevitably talk went back to what was happening at SES — the play.

But this time I didn't wait for Mary Anne and Kristy to get started. "Hey," I said. "Could you guys not talk about the play? It makes me feel left out. And that makes me feel crummy."

Mary Anne's face turned pink. Even Kristy looked surprised.

"It does? But I thought you liked the idea."

"I do. Or I would if I was part of it. But I'm not." I felt a lump come into my throat. "I'm not part of your school anymore."

"You're still our friend," said Mary Anne instantly. She understood what the problem was.

"And you can help us with our plays," said Kristy. "I could ask Ms. Jameson if — "

I shook my head. "No, it's not the same." Then I burst out, "I *hate* going to Stamford. I hate it worse than anything I've ever hated in my life. Those little classes make me feel like the teachers are following me around and watching me all the time."

"Maybe you could talk to your parents," said Kristy. "Tell them how disgusting and yucky Stamford is. Tell them if they'll let you come back to SES you'll work really really hard. Triple harder than you've *ever* worked."

"We could help," said Mary Anne. "We'll tell them that, too."

"Maybe," I said.

"It can't hurt," urged Kristy.

"Maybe," I said again. But I didn't have much hope.

As it turned out, I was right.

I talked to my parents. That night. After dinner. It was a good dinner, so I figured they'd be in a good mood.

"You know, Claudia," said my father before I could even get started, "we've been meaning to talk to you, to tell you how pleased we are with the progress you're making at Stamford."

My mother said, "Wonderful progress, in fact. We're getting such good reports from all your teachers. I know it's been difficult, but you've worked hard. We're both very proud of you."

"But I hate Stamford," I managed to say.

My father frowned. My mother frowned.

"Hate is a strong word, Claudia. Have you given the school a chance? How could you hate a place where you are doing so well?"

"Please let me go back to Stoneybrook," I begged. "All my friends are there. My whole life is there. At Stamford all I do is schoolwork. Soon Mary Anne and Kristy won't be my friends anymore and I won't *have* any friends. It's not worth it. If you let me go back to Stoneybrook, I'll work really, really hard. Triple hard. I'll — "

My father reached out and took my hands in his. "Claudia, settle down. Try to understand it from our point of view. We want what's best for you. We don't want you to feel left behind or not adequate because you perhaps learn at a different pace or in a different way from other kids your own age. At Stamford, that won't happen. You'll learn what you need to learn to get along in the world, to do well. To have a happy future. And if you'll give Stamford a chance, I think you could be happy in the present."

It was hopeless. I could see that. I pulled my hands free of my father's.

"If you'll excuse me," I said. "I have homework to do."

"How's your art project going?" That was my art teacher. She'd never asked me that before. I guess she'd never felt as if she had to.

But then, I'd been sitting in front of a blank piece of posterboard for the last two days, staring at nothing. I'd planned a collage, a "living doll" made up of magazine clippings of elegant models and bits of cloth for clothing and old pieces of jewelry. I was even going to glue one of those scratch-and-sniff perfume ads to the poster.

After my parents had said absolutely no to my going back to SES, I'd lost interest in the project. I guess I'd always thought, in the back of my mind, that if I did really well at SAA, and proved that I could do the work, they'd let me return to my old school. Now it looked as though I were never going back. I was stuck at Stamford Alternative Academy for life.

"Fine," I said. I picked up a model's head that I'd cut out of a magazine and glued it onto the posterboard at random. "Just fine."

I told Kristy and Mary Anne what had happened. Then I told them that I had a lot of extra schoolwork and I couldn't do anything with them for awhile. They continued to call anyway.

But the calls grew fewer and further between as they became more and more involved in their play projects.

I didn't have any extra work. Oh, I had plenty of work to do, don't get me wrong. The work load at SAA was pretty heavy. But that didn't bother me. I'd always worked hard at school, even when I wasn't getting the answers right.

But I had no extra work. I think I'd simply decided, somewhere deep inside, that because I was stuck at SAA, my friendship with Kristy and Mary Anne was through. And instead of letting it die a slow, painful death, it was better to get it over with all at once.

My parents were thrilled with how studious I'd become. I did every homework assignment. I studied for all my tests.

Had I become a mutant Claudia — the world's most perfect student? Was I actually getting hooked on schoolwork because I had nothing else to do?

No. But when I didn't do my work, the response of my new teachers was so unpleasant, it was practically unbearable. They weren't mean. They didn't yell. They didn't hold up papers with big, red, awful marks on them.

Instead, we had conferences.

We talked about why I didn't do my homework, and whether I should tell my parents, or whether I'd be able to "uphold my contract" to do my work without talking to my parents. They asked me for my "input." Was there some approach I could suggest that would be more useful?

They looked hurt.

I hated all that. I hated it because I didn't feel as if they really cared about me. It was as if they were reading from a book about how to deal with a problem student. I wanted to say, fine, tell my parents. That's what you're threatening to do, anyway, isn't it?

But I didn't.

I did my homework.

I came home from school and I went straight upstairs to my room and I did my homework. Then I sat at my desk and stared out the window. Or I lay on my back on the floor with my feet on the side of the bed and stared at the ceiling. Sometimes I just lay on my bed until I fell asleep.

At first my parents were pleased with their perfect little student. But not Mimi. When I didn't sit with her in the kitchen one day for an afternoon snack she came up to my room to see if I was all right. She knocked and I said come in. I'd been sitting at my desk, getting started on my math homework.

"Are you feeling well?" asked Mimi, standing just outside my open door.

"I have a lot of homework," I told her. "And I'm not really hungry."

Mimi's forehead wrinkled. "Maybe when you have finished . . ."

"Yes," I agreed quickly. "As soon as I've finished."

But of course, when I finished I didn't join Mimi. I didn't call Mary Anne or Kristy. I didn't work on my own art projects, or hunt for hidden snacks stored around my room.

I sat there. At first I tried to think, but my brain felt fuzzy, clouded, and gray. After awhile I just sat.

Mimi must have said something to my parents. A few days later, when my mother picked me up after school, she took me out for ice cream.

"Let's be extravagant," she said. "You've worked so hard, you need to play a little. Maybe we could even do a little shopping when we've finished our ice cream."

She ordered a chocolate sundae made with chocolate fudge mint ice cream and double whipped cream and nuts.

I ordered a scoop of vanilla.

"Are you sure?" asked my mother. "I thought you liked pistachio. Or what about a sundae? Or a dipped cone?"

I shrugged. "Vanilla. In a cup."

"So how *is* school?" asked my mom as we sat down with our ice creams.

I shrugged again.

"You're doing very well. Keeping up with your work."

"Yeah."

"But you can't forget your friends. I haven't seen Kristy or Mary Anne around."

"They're busy," I said. "They have a school play."

"That sounds like fun."

"Yes, it sounds like they're having lots of fun," I couldn't resist answering.

We didn't go shopping. (For the first and probably last time in the history of the world I didn't want to shop.) I told my mom I had to do my homework. So we went home. I said hi to Mimi and told her Mom and I had gone to get ice cream, so I wasn't hungry for an after-school snack. Mimi smiled and looked pleased.

I went upstairs to my room. I did my homework. I lay down on my bed and stared at the ceiling until I fell asleep.

It wasn't too long after that when I began to like sleeping an awful lot. One night, I was working on a book report and even though it was way too early for bed, I felt my eyelids drooping. I decided to lie on my bed for just a minute.

The next thing I knew, Mimi was bending over me. "It is time for sleep, my Claudia," she said. "But I see that you have begun."

I couldn't help but smile. I yawned hugely. "Is it late?" I asked. "I was doing my homework and I guess I fell asleep."

"Bedtime," said Mimi.

"I need to finish my book report," I told her. "It won't take long."

She nodded and touched my forehead. "Do not stay up too late."

I didn't. I changed into my pajamas. I looked at the book report. I felt even sleepier than before. So I went back to bed.

The conference I had with my language arts teacher wasn't fun. But I was so out of it that I didn't care. I felt as if I were listening to her from across a valley. I could see her lips move. I could hear her voice. But the words didn't matter.

I didn't quit doing my work in school. I kept gluing things to my collage. But I could see that the collage didn't make any sense. It looked like something a baby would make, scattered fragments that didn't mean anything. My art teacher seemed disturbed. But at least she didn't make me have one of those conferences.

The day after I didn't finish my book report, I fell asleep the moment I got home from school. My father's voice calling "Dinner!" is what woke me.

After dinner I went back upstairs and stared out the window for a long time at the dark. Then I put on my pajamas. When Mimi came to say good night, I was already asleep.

We had more conferences at school. I nodded. I agreed with everything everybody said.

But I couldn't feel anything at all.

My parents came to the school. They had conferences. Then they had a conference with me.

I was sitting at my desk in my room with my book open when my mother and father came in. I wasn't reading. I was staring down at the scramble of letters and words on the page and feeling tired. I was as unhappy as I had ever been in my life.

"You've been doing so well, Claudia," said

not one of my best peaces,
but I think it did captur my mood.

my father. "Don't you want to continue doing well?"

"I guess," I said.

"You can't if you don't do your homework. Your teachers say that you've had conferences with them and agreed to all their suggestions. But you're still not doing your work."

"I'm trying," I said desperately. "I really am."

And it was true.

"Your art teacher said you seem to have lost interest in your project," said my mother.

I looked at my parents. "Art?" I said as if it were a word in another language. "I guess I'm not interested in being an artist anymore."

A small silence followed that announcement. Then my mother said, "Well, I know you've got a lot of work to do. We won't keep you."

When my parents left, I put my head down on my desk. I felt tears slide out of the corner of my eyes and run down my nose onto my arms folded under my head. Quiet, slow, tired tears.

I didn't cry long, though. I just fell asleep.

I wasn't *trying* to fail. I knew that failing at SAA wouldn't mean that I'd get sent back to

SES. I wasn't trying to make my parents or Mimi worry. I wasn't trying to do anything at all. I just didn't care anymore and even the thought of trying to try made me tired and sad.

I don't know how long I felt like that. I remember one Saturday afternoon, my mom knocked on my door and told me I had company. I sat up (I'd been lying on my back with my feet on the bed) and said, "Come in."

Kristy and Mary Anne walked in. "Hey!" Kristy practically shouted. "Long time no see!"

"Hi, Claudia," said Mary Anne softly.

"Hi," I said. Then I couldn't think of anything else to say. I saw my mother hovering in the doorway.

"How is everything?" asked Kristy.

I shrugged. What I wanted to do was lie down again. I thought for a moment. I couldn't think of any reason not to. So I did.

Kristy didn't give up easily. "Have you done any new art projects?" she asked.

"No," I said to the ceiling. "I don't like art anymore."

It was Mary Anne, not Kristy, who spoke loudly this time. "But you love it! More than anything. More than even junk food."

The door closed quietly. My mother had left.

I managed to shrug again, even though I was lying on the floor.

Kristy and Mary Anne tried. They really did. But they didn't stay long. I didn't walk them down the stairs to say good-bye. In my mind, I'd already said good-bye to them a long time before. So I stayed where I was, staring at the ceiling until it was time for dinner. Someday when I grew up maybe I'd have friends again. Maybe I'd take art lessons, too. But until then, I was just fine. All I wanted was to be left alone.

Three days later, I had another after-school conference with my parents and my teachers. I don't remember anything about it, except that I didn't look at anybody and I kept my hands tightly folded in my lap. I agreed with everything everybody said. I didn't know what else to do.

That night, after dinner — a long, quiet dinner — my parents asked me to come into the living room for a talk.

Uh-oh, I thought. I decided I was about to get in Big Trouble. Maybe even be grounded for life.

"Sit down, Claudia," said my mother. She patted the sofa cushion next to her. My father waited until I sat down, then sat in the chair next to me.

Boo for Fourth Grade

My mother took a deep breath. "I have to say I'm disappointed, Claudia. I had such high hopes for Stamford. And you seemed to get off to such a great start."

"But . . ." I began.

My father said, "Exactly. But . . . but although you initially did better academically, you were clearly unhappy, as you told us. Your reluctance to go to a new school and leave all your friends was understandable, but your mother and I thought that would pass, that you would adjust."

"I'm sorry," I mumbled. And I was.

"No, we're sorry. We're sorry this didn't work out because I think it would have made our lives easier in the long run. You need the kind of specialized attention and academic grounding that Stamford offers. But we're also sorry that we didn't realize how difficult such a change would be for you."

I was surprised. I didn't know what to say.

My father leaned over. "Claudia, we've decided that this — experiment — with Stamford Alternative Academy is not working. It is not worth sacrificing you, your happiness, your whole life, for scholastic achievement."

I was surprised. I was stunned. Shocked. Delirious with sudden, unbearable happiness. "Y-you mean it?"

"You will be going back to SES the day after tomorrow. We've made all the arrangements," my mother said.

"Oh, thank you, thank you, thank you!" I shouted. I flung myself at my mom and threw my arms around her neck.

"Whoa," she said. I loosened my hold and grabbed my father.

He laughed and shook his head, loosening my arms. "Claudia, I'm glad to see you so happy. But this change doesn't mean things will be the way they were. We've spoken to your teachers at Stoneybrook and they will be giving you a lot of extra attention — as well as keeping a close eye on you and your work. You will be working with tutors in subjects such as language arts on a regular basis. We're exploring the use of the resource room *and* . . ."

". . . we'll be working with you ourselves at home. Someone will be supervising your homework every night. Agreed?" finished my mom.

"Agreed? Are you kidding! Of course I agree!" I jumped up and practically danced around the living room. Life suddenly wasn't gray and boring and horrible anymore.

I was going back to Stoneybrook. Wait until I told Kristy and Mary Anne. I wondered if there was still time for me to help with the costumes and the scenery in the play. I wondered if I still had some Oreos hidden behind my sock drawer in my room.

I stopped dancing. "Could you excuse me?" I asked breathlessly. "I have to make a couple of phone calls!"

The Sea Rose

As you can tell from my auto-bigraffey, I've known Kristy Thomas almost all my life. I knew she hadn't been crazy about having a baby brother, but that she was crazy about David Michael from the minite he was born. I knew her father had left not long after — I'd even told her I was sorry, altho I had not liked Mr. Thomas very much. Kristy said Its okay, and had never talked about it again. Then the sumer I was eleven, the sumer of the beach vacashun, I began to relize that you can know somone and not know much about them at all . . .

The Sea Rose

The summer we were eleven — Kristy, Mary Anne, and I — Kristy's older brothers Charlie and Sam were part of a super good baseball team. Their team made the play-offs, which were being held a couple of hours from Stoneybrook in this totally remote corner of Connecticut called Hammond Beach. Charlie and Sam were psyched about it, and so was Kristy. She'd been playing catch and softball and baseball with her brothers practically ever since she could walk.

The play-offs were going to be held over a four-day weekend, from Thursday through Sunday, and Kristy was dying to go. At first her mom had said maybe they could go to Hammond Beach on the Saturday or the Sunday of the play-offs. Mary Anne and I had said we wanted to go, too, and Kristy had started making plans for the Big Day Trip to Hammond Beach. Then Mary Anne found out that she and her father were going to visit relatives that week. And then . . .

"Guess what!" Kristy screamed in my ear. I almost dropped the phone.

"I guess that you're shouting," I said, holding the phone at a safe distance.

"Oh. Sorry. Guess what? We're going to Hammond Beach for the *whole* weekend! All four days. We get to see Charlie and Sam's team win the playoffs *and* we get to vacation at the beach."

"Cool," I said.

"It is. Super duper cool! And guess what else! I get to invite someone to come with me. You want to come?"

"Yes!" I said. "I mean, I have to ask my parents, but yes, yes, yes, I want to go!"

"Ask them the moment they get home and call me back," Kristy ordered. "My mom can tell them all the stuff they need to know."

My mom and dad talked it over and agreed, and then my mom talked to Mrs. Thomas. I kept swooping through the kitchen, where Mom was on the phone making a list and saying, "Mmm. Okay. Yes, we'll do that . . ."

Then she finally hung up and said, "Well."

"Well," said my mom again, smiling. "You're going to the beach next week, Claudia Kishi. We've got quite a bit of planning and packing to do."

I'd never been away with another family. (I didn't count sleepovers at Kristy's and Mary Anne's.) I was excited and nervous. Would I be homesick? Would Charlie and Sam tease me? What if I was homesick and they found out about it and made fun of me for being a baby? And what should I pack?

Mom had made a basic list with Mrs. Thomas: towels, a pillow, sunscreen, etc. I talked Mom into a new bathing suit and a cool pair of sunglasses. I also let all the air out of an old beach float and squeezed it into my suitcase. Plus a couple of Nancy Drew books, plus some snacks (just in case).

My mom put in sunscreen, a beach hat, extra underwear, extra socks, a pair of long pants, and a windbreaker. I added shorts and about a million T-shirts, plus sandals.

As you might guess, I could barely get my suitcase squeezed shut. But I managed. My mom also gave me money. "If we forgot to pack anything, you can buy it when you get there," she told me. "It's not as if you're going to the end of the world."

That was a comforting thought and made me feel a little less nervous. But all the same I could hardly sleep the night before I left, and I ran to the Thomases' with my suitcase practically at the crack of dawn the next day.

I wasn't the only one who was up, packed, and ready. Kristy met me at the door and I could see the line of suitcases and bags of baseball gear crammed into the front hall. "We already took Louie to the kennel where he's staying," she said. "Come on. Hurry."

"Uh-oh," I said, dragging my bulging suitcase into the house. "How will we ever all fit in the car?"

"We're going to tie David Michael to the luggage rack on the roof of the station wagon," said Kristy.

"Nooo!" cried David Michael, who was five then. He'd come trotting into the hall behind Kristy. But he was grinning and I could tell it was a joke she'd made with him before.

For a little while, chaos reigned as the Thomas family took luggage to the car, along with all the other things they needed for the trip. And I was almost beginning to believe that one of us would have to ride on the roof. But in the end, we squeezed into the car and took off for Hammond Beach.

Kristy and I sat in the backseat of the station wagon, the one that folded down and faced backward out the rear window. Our feet were propped up on a mountain of stuff and other stuff was squeezed in on either side of us. Charlie sat in the front with Mrs. Thomas and Sam and David Michael sat in the back.

"Hey, Kristy, Claudia!" Charlie shouted. "Quit making faces! You're gonna cause the cars behind us to wreck."

"We're not making faces," I said indignantly.

"You're not? You mean your regular faces are causing all the cars to swerve?" teased Charlie.

Kristy rolled her eyes. "Family resemblance, Charlie," she called back. "How do you know it's not *your* face?"

Sam cracked up and so did Kristy. I couldn't think of anything to say, but I had to grin. Kristy was tough.

We played the alphabet game with license plates (going through the alphabet looking for the different letters on the tags of cars). Kristy and Charlie and Sam joked and teased each other during the entire trip.

When we stopped for gas, Charlie pumped it and Mrs. Thomas consulted her map and Kristy and I got sodas while Sam took David Michael to the restroom. Somewhere, Sam got a piece of ice and slipped it down Kristy's back, making her shriek. But Kristy went Sam one better. As he was leaning over to strap David Michael back into his seatbelt in the car, Kristy slipped ice down Sam's pants.

David Michael thought that was even funnier than when Kristy had shrieked about the ice down her back. Mrs. Thomas smiled as if she were used to that sort of thing happening all the time (I guess in the Thomases' house it did) and I got back into the car next to Kristy, glad that I didn't have any older brothers always teasing me. Janine might be a pain, but at least she was a quiet pain.

It was a fun trip, though. And it seemed

like no time at all before we reached a sign that said "Hammond Beach, 21 miles." We turned off the highway down a two-lane road that wound in and out among woods and rocky fields. We passed roadside stands that sold fresh fruit and vegetables as well as beach souvenirs and funny hats. Mrs. Thomas stopped and bought a watermelon at one of the stands for dessert that night (Kristy and I rode the rest of the way with the watermelon under our feet). Then more and more houses began to appear and suddenly we went around a curve and saw a sign that said "Hammond Beach."

Witch way to the BEACH?!?!

Chapter 13

I'd been to the beach before. So I expected a big, busy beach town, full of tourists and cars and lots of shops and games such as putt-putt golf. But Hammond Beach wasn't that big or busy. The street we drove in on was called Hammond Main, because it was the main street in town. I found out later that it ran straight to the beach parking lot at the end of town and stopped there. I saw some tourist shops along Main, but it looked pretty normal: grocery stores, an old-fashioned Woolworth's, and a hardware store. As we drove into town, we passed a big, white columned hotel set in the middle of a green lawn. We went through town and turned down a side road and passed several motels along the beach road. They were mostly two stories high and made of cedar, although a couple were made of cement and painted bright tropical colors. A lot of them had tennis courts and most of them had swimming pools. One of them, a gleaming white motel, had a sign out front that advertised Jacuzzis in the rooms. Another, made up of separate units shaped like ski chalets, another offered a free movie channel.

We kept driving. The road grew narrower and turned into rocky dirt. Then Mrs. Thomas said, "Here we are!" and pulled over to a small, low one-story building set right on the dirt road. The only thing between the doors of the rooms and the road was the parking lot.

No tennis court. No swimming pool. For sure no Jacuzzis or free movie channels. It was painted a faded pink. The sign out front said "Sea Rose." I guess that explained the color.

Mrs. Thomas went inside and registered, and came out holding a handful of keys. "We're down at the end," she said. "It'll be nice and private. We have two adjoining rooms, one for the girls and one for the boys. One room is a kitchenette, so we can cook. *And* both rooms have private baths."

No one else seemed to notice how rundown and plain the Sea Rose was. And I guess it didn't really matter. Inside it was clean and comfortable. Kristy and I were going to share a double bed and Mrs. Thomas took the other bed. The kitchenette was on the oceanside, a tiny oven and refrigerator with a narrow divider between it and the sleeping area. Two stools stood on one side of the divider. The bathroom opened off the narrow kitchen walkway. The front window was small and partially blocked by a huge, ancient air-conditioner. The back wall had another window that looked out onto the ocean and next to it was a back door that opened onto a walkway that led to a path down to the beach.

"Cool," I said, the moment I opened the door.

As you might have guessed, Kristy and I were out of our shorts and into our bathing suits in almost no time.

Mrs. Thomas looked at her watch. "Charlie and Sam need to go for a practice in just a little while and we need to find the playing fields. Do you want to come with us or — "

"The beach!" said Kristy.

Mrs. Thomas smiled. "I thought so. Okay, but I'm going to leave you in charge of David Michael. We won't be gone long. I'll take Sam and Charlie, do some grocery shopping, and then come back. We can fix lunch then. Mrs. Acqui, who owns the Sea Rose, said to call her if we need anything. There's a phone in the office and a soda machine and ice machine, too."

"Great," said Kristy. She banged on the door to the boys' room. "David Michael, get moving!" I heard her shout. "We're going to the beach!"

We didn't even wait to wave good-bye to the Thomases. With Kristy in charge, we were on our way down the steps to the beach in no time flat.

It wasn't a big, sweeping ocean beach. It was narrow and rocky. Apparently, people didn't just come to Hammond Beach to lie in the sun. Not too far out I could see two small boats with people fishing from them. A little way up the beach, a man and a boy were exploring an outcropping of rocks along the shore. But further along, where the bigger hotels began, was a short boardwalk, with umbrellas above hot-dog and soda stands.

"This is great!" I said, turning my face up to the sun.

"Don't forget the sunscreen," said Kristy. She was already slathering it on David Michael with one hand, holding him still with the other.

"I'm not going to get sunburned!" David Michael whined.

"That's right, you're not," said Kristy, adding another layer of sunblock to his ears and neck.

At last she let him go and we decided to take a walk down the beach. Of course, David Michael spotted the umbrellas and immediately wanted to buy a hot dog. Kristy wouldn't let him, though.

"Mom said we'd have lunch when she got back," Kristy told him. "Eating a hot dog now would spoil your appetite. Besides, what if she buys hot dogs for us to cook for lunch?"

Poking out his lower lip, David Michael said, "I'm hungry now!"

"Maybe we could all split something," I suggested. (I was secretly impressed by how grown-up and responsible Kristy seemed.)

"Maybe," said Kristy. We walked in the direction of the boardwalk and the town beach. We passed the hot-dog stand and another cart selling sodas and ice cream. Suddenly Kristy pointed. A sign said "QuiK MarKet" and an arrow pointed to a flight of stairs up from the boardwalk to the road.

We climbed the stairs and crossed the road (we'd reached the paved section, but there was no traffic to be seen in either direction). In the QuiK MarKet Kristy surveyed the merchandise and steered David Michael toward the ice-cream section. I was surprised until she pointed to the Frozfruit pops, which are made out of fruit juice. "You can have any flavor you want," she told David Michael.

"Really?" David Michael was delighted, and considered for at least ten minutes before choosing a strawberry Frozfruit. I got a Ben &

Jerry's Peace Pop. Kristy got a soda.

We walked back to the beach with our treats and sat on a rock at the water's edge to finish them. It was a calm day and the waves weren't very high. The clouds were big and white and puffy and it wasn't too hot or too old. It was just right.

"This is *super*," I said.

Kristy grinned. "Triple super," she agreed.

David Michael didn't say anything. He was busy making sure his Frozfruit didn't melt before he finished it.

When we got back to the motel, Mrs. Thomas had just returned. We helped her unload groceries from the car, and then made lunch (and there were hot dogs for David Michael and Kristy and me). Soon Mrs. Thomas had to leave to pick up Charlie and Sam. Kristy convinced David Michael to take a nap in our room while she and I sat on chairs on the little strip of walk outside the back door and read magazines.

After David Michael's nap we got out my old float and some of the other floats that Kristy's mom had brought and started blowing them up. I was glad when Sam and Charlie got back to help. The blowing made me dizzy.

That night we cooked spaghetti in the tiny kitchen. It was a lot of fun and everybody pitched in, even David Michael, who was in charge of setting the table and adding the spices. Mrs. Thomas made a big batch so it would last several days. Afterward, we took the watermelon to the beach, spread out a blanket, sat on it, and ate watermelon until the sun went down.

So far, I liked Hammond Beach. And I wasn't homesick one bit.

The next morning, Charlie and Sam were off to the first round of the play-offs. Even though I knew Kristy was dying to go with them, she offered to stay at the Sea Rose and take care of David Michael. "He'd get bored if he had to go to all of the play-offs," she told her mom. "We'll go on Saturday or Sunday for the whole day."

"Or maybe both days," said her mother, looking relieved. "Are you sure you don't mind?"

"Nope," said Kristy. She grinned at me. "I bet Claud doesn't mind having to spend the day at the beach either. Do you, Claud?"

I had to admit that the beach would have been my first choice.

"If you swim," said Mrs. Thomas, "go down to the town beach where there's a life-guard."

"Okay," said Kristy. "We're going to take our floats today."

"We'll be back for a late lunch," said Mrs. Thomas. "Sam and Charlie only have one game today."

"Great. Come on, Claud. Let's hurry. I want to get a good place on the beach."

We wished Charlie and Sam good luck and then headed for the town beach.

"Are there sharks?" asked David Michael, surveying the water suspiciously.

"No," Kristy told him firmly.

"Why not?" he asked.

"Because we have a lifeguard. The lifeguard watches out for sharks." I pointed to the woman sitting on the lifeguard stand.

"She can see sharks? Wow!" David Michael made a beeline for the lifeguard stand. By the time we caught up with him, he was holding on to the stand, waving up at the lifeguard.

"Can you see sharks?" asked David Michael.

The lifeguard leaned over and smiled down at David Michael. "I've only seen one shark and I've been here two summers," she said.

"Did it *eat* someone?"

"David Michael!" said Kristy in exasperation.

The lifeguard smiled and shook her head. "It was just swimming by. The beach wasn't crowded, and I asked everybody to get out of the water for a little while, just in case."

Nodding seriously, David Michael said, "If you ever say, 'Everyone get out of the water,' *I* will."

"He's my little brother," explained Kristy. "He's four."

"And a half," said David Michael. I hid a smile.

"Well, you do what your sister tells you," the lifeguard said. "And all three of you obey the rules for the beach, okay?" She pointed to a sign by her chair.

We nodded and Kristy read the rules aloud to David Michael.

We spent the morning playing on the floats in the shallow water near the shore. David Michael had not been in the Atlantic Ocean before that he could remember (although Kristy said her mom had pictures of him at the shore on the Long Island Sound when he was just a baby). When we grew tired of splashing in the water, we got out and spread our towels on the beach. Kristy coated her little brother in another layer of sunblock and made him put his hat on. Then she settled him down with his shovel and a bucket. "If you build a good castle," she told him, "maybe we can go collect some shells and rocks to decorate it with."

That was fine with David Michael, who was, I could tell, tired from all the splashing and sun and excitement. He went to work.

Kristy surveyed the beach. "Too bad there aren't any other kids here who are David Michael's age," she said.

"It's a weekday," I reminded her. "More families with kids will probably show up on the weekend."

"Yeah." Kristy smiled ruefully. "But I want to watch Charlie and Sam play at least once."

"You will," I said.

When we returned to the motel, Charlie and Sam were bouncing off the walls with excitement. "You won?" asked Kristy.

"It was a *great* game," said Charlie jubilantly. "The team is going out for pizza tonight. Mom, can you give us a ride to the pizza parlor? Then we can get a ride back with someone afterward."

I knew some of the team was staying at a hotel farther up the beach. Mrs. Thomas smiled. "Sure," she said.

We all spent the afternoon out at the beach and had a great time. When it was time for David Michael's nap, Charlie took him to the Sea Rose and stayed with him. "I could use some rest, too," he told David Michael.

Kristy and me at the beech.
Acting not so grown-up.

Kristy and I got to hang out on the beach on our own. We walked up and down and tried to look much older than we were (I don't think we succeeded). That night, Mrs. Thomas asked Kristy to stay with David Michael for just half an hour while she took Charlie and Sam to the pizza parlor.

"No problem," said Kristy.

"Right," I said. I thought it was cool the way Mrs. Thomas left Kristy in charge. Most families would have hired a mother's helper for the trip, but I guessed Mrs. Thomas couldn't afford one. And she didn't need one, either. Kristy was being super responsible. And so was I.

Mrs. Thomas came back with pizza for all of us. Dinner was a lot of fun. I ate as much pizza as I could hold and then Kristy and I got permission to walk to the boardwalk for ice-cream cones after David Michael had gone to bed. We hung over the railing of the boardwalk, watching people, until the last possible minute before we had to leave. Then we ran all the way back to the Sea Rose.

The next day Kristy's brothers had two games, a morning and an afternoon game. Mrs. Thomas, David Michael, Kristy, and I went to the morning game. David Michael had fun for awhile, cheering for his brothers and listening to Kristy's explanations of the plays. But then he became restless. I offered to walk around with him and Kristy threw me a grateful look.

"Would you? Super. It's only two more innings."

I wasn't all that interested in baseball, but I figured two innings wouldn't be long. So David Michael and I walked around the field beyond the outfield until I heard cheering that I knew meant the end of the game.

That afternoon after lunch, Kristy and I stayed at the Sea Rose with David Michael.

"I'll have to be more prepared tomorrow," Kristy said. "Although if they win their game this afternoon, they only have one game tomorrow. And if they win that one, they have one game on Sunday morning. I'm going to see *both* of those."

"Why don't we see if we can find some games for David Michael to play when he gets bored?" I suggested. "And maybe some books. I can read to him while the game is going on."

"You don't mind? That's a great idea, Claud."

Naturally we decided to put the plan into action right away. Kristy went to the QuiK MarKet while I stayed with David Michael, who was taking his nap in his room. It was my first real baby-sitting job and I took it very seriously. Every five minutes I cracked the door to David Michael's room and peeked in. He never moved and before I knew it, Kristy was back.

"Did you find good stuff?"

She wrinkled her nose. "It was sort of expensive. But I found some pick-up sticks and a magnetic go-fish game."

"He'll love that."

"And a deck of cards. He loves playing slap jack."

We both laughed.

Soon after, David Michael woke up and we went down to the beach in front of the motel. For awhile we worked on a sand castle, molding turrets with the cups and pots and pans from the Sea Rose kitchenette (Kristy figured it was okay as long as we washed them out afterward).

Then David Michael decided that he *had* to have a hot dog.

"Please, please, please," he begged.

"Wellll," said Kristy (sounding just like somebody's mother).

"Pleeeeeeease," said David Michael.

"Okay. I guess one hot dog won't ruin your dinner. It's still a long way away. You can go. But don't go in the water."

"I won't," David Michael promised.

"And be back in ten minutes. That's *very soon*. Do you understand?"

"Yes, I will," said David Michael. He took off like a shot. We watched as he raced down the beach, waving at the lifeguard as he went by. He was still going at top speed as he flew up the steps to the boardwalk where the hot-dog stand was.

"Maybe naps really do give you energy," I said thoughtfully.

"I wish I'd asked him to get a soda for me," said Kristy. She yawned.

Time passed. Kristy looked at her watch. "It's been ten minutes," she said. She looked toward the concession stand. "I don't see David Michael, do you?"

"Not yet. But he probably stopped to eat the hot dog," I said.

"In one bite," said Kristy. "He's a hot-dog eating machine! He learned *that* from Charlie and Sam. They think eating three hot dogs for dinner is great."

We made faces and giggled. I told Kristy that my sister's favorite food was broccoli. For some reason, that made us laugh even harder.

But suddenly Kristy stopped laughing. She

looked at her watch. She stood up and scanned the beach.

"Claudia," she said, her voice low and worried. "I don't see David Michael anywhere. And it's been more than twenty minutes since he left."

"Twenty minutes," I said. "That isn't so long, Kristy. He's probably . . ." My voice trailed off. I knew David Michael only had enough money for a hot dog. What could he be doing? Window shopping at the ice-cream stand?

Or worse, had he crossed the street by himself to the QuiK MarKet? Or even worse . . .

I couldn't help it. I looked out at the ocean. All that water. Surely David Michael hadn't decided to go swimming by himself.

If I was thinking that way, I knew Kristy had to be, too.

"Let's go check the shops on the boardwalk," I said. "Starting with the hot-dog stand."

Without a word, Kristy started racing toward the boardwalk. I followed her.

No one was standing under the red and yellow umbrella of the hot-dog stand.

"Have you seen a little boy, about this tall," Kristy held her hand out just below her chest, "with dark hair? He's five and he bought a hot dog from you about twenty minutes ago?"

"With everything on it, and I do mean everything," the man said. He laughed. "I said, 'You want relish *and* onions and sauerkraut?' And he said, 'And ketchup and mustard, too.' Kid had a strong stomach. I sell good hot dogs, don't get me wrong, they wouldn't make you sick, but — "

"Excuse me," said Kristy, trying to sound polite, "but where did he go after he bought the hot dog?"

"Sat down and ate it." The man laughed again. He didn't seem at all curious why we were asking questions. "Said he wished he could buy another one. All my customers should be like that!"

"Did he leave after that?"

"I guess so," the man told Kristy. "Some other customers came up, so I couldn't really say."

"If he comes back, would you tell him to go straight back to his motel?" asked Kristy.

"Sure," said the man. "Want to buy a hot dog?"

"No, *thank you,*" I said, grabbing Kristy's elbow. "Come on."

We hurried down the boardwalk, looking in all the food stands and snack bars and souvenir shops. No David Michael anywhere.

"Maybe he went to the QuiK MarKet," I said at last. "The street's not very busy and he knows to look both ways."

"He *knows* not to cross the street *at all* by himself," said Kristy with gritted teeth. But she led the way to the QuiK MarKet, barely stopping to look both ways herself.

No David Michael.

I was beginning to panic. And if I was, I knew Kristy must be about to go out of her mind.

We hurried back toward the beach. When we reached the top of the stairs down to the town beach, Kristy stopped so abruptly that I crashed into her.

"Sorry," I said.

Kristy pointed with a shaking hand. I looked in the direction she was pointing. The lifeguard was hurtling across the sand at top speed. A crowd of people had gathered at the water's edge, pointing and shouting.

I thought, Oh, my lord, a shark is eating David Michael! As you can tell, I wasn't thinking very clearly at this point.

Kristy launched herself down the stairs just as the lifeguard dove into the water.

"She got her," a woman's voice sobbed just as we reached the crowd.

"Her," I said to Kristy urgently, grabbing her elbow and yanking hard. "Her, Kristy. It's not David Michael."

Another lifeguard had raced out into the water to meet the first and the two of them were guiding in a little girl, clutching her floating duck. The little girl was screaming.

A woman fell on her knees in the sand by the little girl and grabbed her. "Baby, are you okay?"

"I think she's okay. She just drifted out too far," said the lifeguard. She'd bent over and was panting for air. "Got scared."

Kristy turned a pale face toward me. "If it's not David Michael, then where is he?" she said. "He's been gone almost an hour now. We should get some help, tell someone."

"The police?" I said in alarm.

Nodding grimly, Kristy said, "And the lifeguards, too. We can't take any chances."

Then her voice broke. I totally freaked out. I'd hardly ever seen Kristy cry.

"Kristy? It'll be all right."

"If anything happens to David Michael, it'll be all my fault," she said.

"Let's look one more time. We'll split up. You go that way and I'll go this way." I pointed to opposite ends of the beach.

After a moment Kristy nodded. "If we don't find him in ten minutes, though, we meet back at the lifeguard stand."

"Right," I said. I took off.

I raced down the beach, looking wildly from one side to the other. Kids in the surf, kids building sand castles, couples asleep in the sun, families having picnics under beach umbrellas.

No David Michael.

I looked at my watch. Time had run out. I turned and ran back toward the lifeguard stand, my heart pounding with fear.

And just as I reached the stand, I heard Kristy shout, "CLAUDIA!"

From the very fartherest end of the town beach, I saw her waving her arms wildly. I sprinted toward her. As I drew closer I saw her leap forward and grab a little boy by the arm.

David Michael.

"David Michael, where have you been?" Kristy yelled at the top of her lungs. I came to a stop and tried to catch my breath as David Michael pulled his arm free of Kristy's grip.

"Why are you yelling?" he asked. "She's my big sister," he said to two other kids about his age who were playing in the sand with him.

"Hi," said one of the kids. The other nodded

and continued to excavate a hole under one wall of the castle.

"Because you were supposed to be back in ten minutes. *TEN MINUTES!* Do you know how long it's been? It's been over an *hour*."

That got David Michael's attention. "Are my ten minutes up?" He stood up. " 'Bye," he said to the other two kids.

" 'Bye," they replied.

Then David Michael looked at Kristy. Her face was red. Her eyes were very bright. I decided she could go either way: burst into tears or explode.

Maybe David Michael did, too. He said simply, "I'm sorry."

That did it. Kristy threw her arms around her little brother and hugged him hard.

"Hey," protested David Michael. "Let me go!"

Kristy did. Then she said, "Don't you ever, ever do that again, David Michael. Do you hear me? Don't you ever say you're going somewhere and then not come straight back."

"Okay," said David Michael.

The three of us began to walk along the beach.

"What am I going to tell Mom?" said Kristy as we reached the motel. "We're going to be in so much trouble."

My heart sank. If Kristy got in trouble, so

would I. Especially if my parents found out.

But David Michael shrugged. "Don't tell her," he said. "If you tell her, I'll get in trouble, too. And I didn't mean to do anything wrong!"

Quickly I said, "That's true. And Kristy, no one would ever know anything happened."

Kristy frowned. "I should tell Mom," she said.

"Why? We've all learned our lesson. It'll just make her worry," I argued. "If she doesn't ask, we don't have to tell."

David Michael and I watched Kristy anxiously. At last she nodded. "Okay," she said.

I nodded. David Michael nodded.

"It's our secret, forever," said Kristy. "We tell no one, not even Mary Anne."

"Deal," I said.

"Deal," said David Michael solemnly.

David Michael decided to take another little nap.

Kristy and I decided to take a nap, too.

We were exhausted.

But, I thought, Kristy must have been the tiredest of all. She'd been responsible for David Michael for most of the trip. Her mother relied on her a lot. And she stood up to her older brothers' teasing without even flinching.

No wonder Kristy was tough. In that short vacation, I'd gotten to know Kristy much better. And my respect and admiration for her had grown tremendously. I had known Kristy all my life, but it had never occurred to me that it might not be easy being Kristin Amanda Thomas. She was doing a super job.

When I'd finished writing my autobiography, I made it into a book. I typed it into Janine's computer. (Which wasn't so bad. Maybe I'd let my parents get me a computer, too, after all. I'd always avoided it before. It seemed like a way of getting me to do more schoolwork, somehow.) Then Janine showed me how to pick special type so my story would look more booklike. I even left spaces at the beginning of each chapter so I could write the chapter numbers in.

I made a special design for each chapter. I also added some of my artwork and pasted in some photographs. Then I made a table of contents listing the chapters and their corresponding pages. Finally I drew a self-portrait for the cover: a new version of the butterfly I'd drawn as my self-portrait in first grade.

And I even made a dedication page: *To Mimi*.

I'd started out not liking my project. But I ended up doing more work on it than I ever imagined. I learned a lot, too. I remembered things I hadn't thought about in a long time. I realized that I'd made a lot of progress over the years. That I really was growing up. Changing. Learning new things.

I even understood why people thought learning history was so important. Remembering my history had taught me a lot. The mistakes I'd made were mistakes I wouldn't make again. And the things I'd done right were things I could be proud of.

And I realized, too, just how lucky I was: I had a great family and great friends.

Still, when I handed my autobiography in, I didn't expect great things. One of the things I've learned about school is that even when I try hard, I don't necessarily do well. Another thing I've learned (from my parents telling me about a million times, and from Mimi, and from my own experience) is that if I've done my best, it doesn't matter what grade is at the top of a project.

As soon as I handed my autobiography in, though, I started on another autobiography, an art project: a series of self-portraits of me as I remember myself and as I see myself now.

For the last self-portrait, I was going to show how I imagined myself when I was grown-up.

It would be interesting to look back at that one the same way I now looked back at my butterfly portrait from first grade.

I got so involved in my artist autobiographical series that I actually forgot about the autobiography I'd written for school. So when the teacher handed mine back to me, I held it for a moment as if it were something brand new.

At last I opened it. And I couldn't help smiling.

The teacher had given me a B–. "An A+ for content and design, Claudia," she'd written across the top of the first page. "Very impressive. But you still need to work on organization, grammar, and spelling. Keep up the good work!"

My parents would be pleased. I was pleased, too. But as I said, the grade wasn't so important. I'd learned what I needed to know.

And when I was a famous artist, maybe I'd write another autobiography. . . .

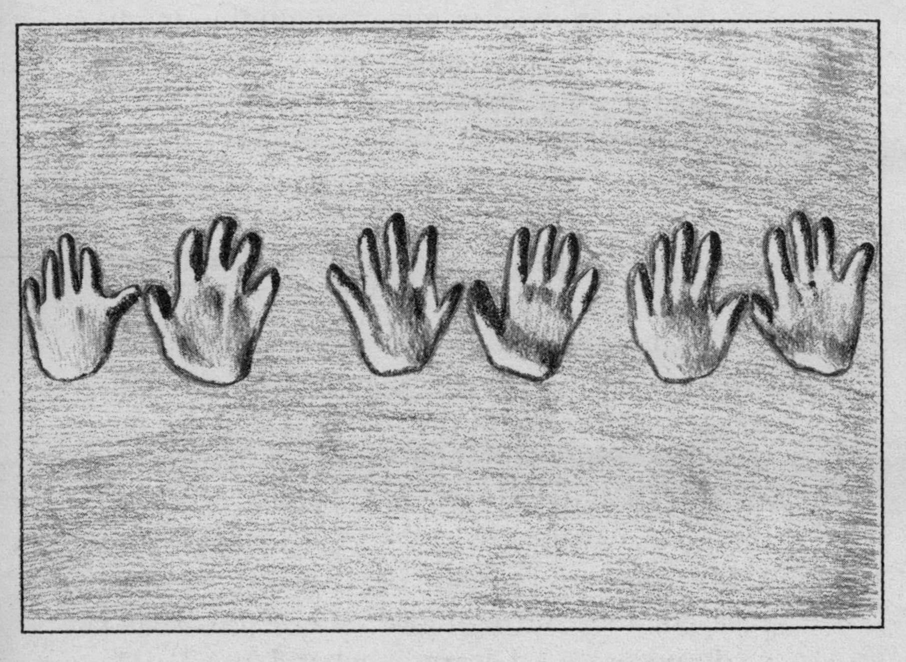

Hand prints in the cement of time --
with thanks to Mimi.

About the Author

ANN M. MARTIN did *a lot* of baby-sitting when she was growing up in Princeton, New Jersey. She is a former editor of books for children, and was graduated from Smith College.

Ms. Martin lives in New York City with her cats, Mouse and Rosie. She likes ice cream and *I Love Lucy*; and she hates to cook.

Ann Martin's Apple Paperbacks include *Yours Turly, Shirley*; *Ten Kids, No Pets*; *With You and Without You*; *Bummer Summer*; and all the other books in the Baby-sitters Club series.

More titles... ➧

Create Your Own Mystery Stories!

MYSTERY GAME!

WHO:	Boyfriend	**WHY:**	Romance
WHAT:	Phone Call	**WHERE:**	Dance

Use the special Mystery Case card to pick WHO did it, WHAT was involved, WHY it happened and WHERE it happened. Then dial secret words on your Mystery Wheels to add to the story! Travel around the special Stoneybrook map gameboard to uncover your friends' secret word clues! Finish four baby-sitting jobs and find out all the words to win. Then have everyone join in to tell the story!

**YOU'LL FIND THIS
GREAT MILTON BRADLEY GAME
AT TOY STORES AND BOOKSTORES
NEAR YOU!**

Wow! It's really them-
the new Baby-sitters Club dolls!

Your favorite Baby-sitters Club characters have come to life in these beautiful collector dolls. Each doll wears her own unique clothes and jewelry. They look just like the girls you have imagined! The dolls also come with their own individual stories in special edition booklets that you'll find nowhere else.

Look for the new Baby-sitters Club collection...
coming soon to a store near you!

Kenner®

The purchase of this item will result in a donation to the Ann M. Martin Foundation, dedicated to benefiting children, education and literacy programs, and the homeless.